THOSE WE LOVE

&

WHAT THEY HIDE

I hope you enjoy the book!

J. Marie

-- A NOVEL --

Written by: J. Marie

This book is a work of fiction. Any references to historical events, real people, or real places are used fictitiously. Other names, characters, places, and events are products of the author's imagination, and any resemblance to actual events or places or persons, living or dead, is entirely coincidental.

THOSE WE LOVE & WHAT THEY HIDE by J. Marie
Copyright 2020, J. Marie

www.jmariebooks.com

Cover Photography by Douglas Bergeson © Winding Road-Bavaria
Cover art by Kelley Nemitz & Katie Eney 2020

Natalie

I dream that I have emerged from under the stifling cloak of heavy water that weighs down my body and I now walk on firm ground again.

But I know up there I would be wandering, lost in those trees, knowing that I am supposed to be somewhere, but unable to find the place.

I would be wandering. Scared and alone. Alone. And, scared.

Above me, up there, the crunch of twigs under the weight of a fresh snow cover, the crackling caw of a black bird, the low, slow whistle of the wind as it creeps through the Douglas firs, it's always the same, it's so very still.

Day in, day out.

That place where nature and man don't often meet -there, the slightest hitch of your breath will draw the sharp-eyed interest of the owl perched on the branch above or divert the vigilant timber wolf off the path of his hunt.

But I'm not really up there on firm ground. I am down here. I am lost down here. It feels like I have been lost here forever.

If only I had left a trail - maybe then I would have a chance for someone to find me.

But, as my Georgia-born mother used to say, that is a fanciful thought and my chance for fanciful thoughts has long since passed.

So, I will wait here another day, another year.

Rest assured, someone will find me someday and finally, I will tell my secrets. Someday.

CHAPTER 1

April 2019

Henri

The tires of the mud-spattered yellow school bus plowed trenches 2-inches deep into the wet gravel as it turned onto the driveway. Cutting through dense woods, eventually, the bus emerged into the dappled sunlight of Henri's front yard. The long needles that were shed from the towering Norway pine trees blanketed the yard and allowed only the most ardent patches of bright green, spring grass to reach the sunlight. Along with a few random bushes and over-size rock outcrops, the natural elements melded into a patchwork of color on either side of the flat, stone walkway which led to the low-slung cedar-sided home crafted to blend into the landscape of the gently sloped yard.

Always happy to be home after school, Henri waved to a few friends as he skipped down the aisle of the bus, avoiding the assortment of back packs and tennis shoes spilling into it. As the heavy bus door clapped shut behind him, he dodged a few puddles in the driveway and scaled the front steps of the expansive, covered porch with the wicker rocking chairs and let himself in the front door.

His house was usually empty when he got home from school, but it was familiar and welcoming with its pleasant blend of smells including spent wood from the wood-burning fireplace and drifts of the laundry detergent his mom used for their clothes. When the weather was nice outside like it was today, he did not want to stay in the empty house anyway. He couldn't wait to get outside to play.

On a mission to do just that, Henri tossed his backpack into the corner of the mudroom, swept open the closet door and quickly scanned the closet's contents in search of his snowshoes. He might not need snowshoes today - it was warm, and the snow was melting fast. But like Poppy always said, better safe than sorry.

Henri emptied his backpack onto the mudroom floor into a mess of papers, including his Math homework that was a day late, and some yellow pencils. He stuffed the snowshoes inside the empty bag and zipped up the sides as far as they would go. As he trudged across the wide-planked, rustic hardwood floor towards the kitchen, he glanced at the wet soles of his snow boots and considered the consequences.

"It's only water. Mom won't be too mad," he thought to himself with an almost-guilty-feeling shrug.

Quickly moving past the feeling, he proceeded into the kitchen, slathered peanut butter and jelly onto bread, grabbed a bottle of water and an apple from the refrigerator and placed it all in a zip lock bag. As he nestled the lunch into the large front pocket of his backpack, he noticed his cell phone resting under a few crunched school lunch notices and some spare change.

Sliding his finger over the screen, Henri checked the phone to see if his mom had texted him yet.

She hadn't.

Good. He still had time.

Reaching for his binoculars that hung by the back door, Henri placed them carefully into the backpack and slung it over his shoulder. After clicking the back door shut, he pulled on his knit stocking hat and mittens and skipped down the steps and across the wide yard in search of the beaver.

During the past few days, the snow at school in Twin Shores had started to melt, there were huge puddles everywhere and the principal had called indoor recess for the past two days because he said the playground was too saturated for them to play on it.

But at home, Henri's yard still had drifts three feet high, even more in spots under the thick evergreens. Most years, here inside the woods, it was mid-May before all the snow was gone.

For the first few minutes of his walk, the snowpack was solid, weathered hard from the wind and the cycle of melt and freeze. But, as he trudged deeper into the thick trees, where the snow was more protected, he found his weight was too much for the drifts. His steps were breaking through to his knees and he felt the trickle of ice water in one of his boots.

Finding a large rock popping out of a drift next to a white pine tree filled with fat, spikey pinecones, Henri sat down on the cold surface and attached the snowshoes. It was slower going with snowshoes, and the lift/slide motion made his legs ache after a while, but he was still glad he'd brought them. Not much further now anyway, he told himself.

It was hard to tell how far a walk it was from his house to the river coming this way, from the north. The trees were thick and there weren't many open spaces to see the road from this angle. Each time he glimpsed the road though, he'd hold his breath hoping that he wouldn't see the gray van with the blue stripe from the memory center where his grandpa spent his days while his mom was at work. He loved his grandpa, whom he called Poppy, and most days he looked forward to seeing Poppy when they dropped him off. Today though, he needed a little more time to himself.

A few minutes later, it was the sound – that low rushing growl of the river - that made his heart rate quicken and he smiled as the sun peaked through the thick, green canopy above him. Finally, he was here!

The sun bounced off the rock cliff and had warmed the ground under his feet into a thick sludge of pine needles, leaves and damp earth. Henri sat down as silently as he could, removed his snowshoes and retrieved the binoculars from his backpack. Gripping them carefully in his mitten so they wouldn't slip out of his hand, he laid stomach-down on the rock and shimmied his way to the edge while glancing over, careful not to crumble any small rocks over the edge to give away his position.

This is where he saw the beaver last Saturday afternoon. Henri sat mesmerized that day as the river tossed around all sorts of winter trash like thick clumps of roots attached to hefty tree stumps, heavy round rocks and large chunks of snow-packed ice. The constant barrage of floating trash crashed into and around the beaver dam that sat just below this rock cliff. But the two beavers that called the dam home didn't seem to notice the chaos around them at all as they spent the afternoon moving in and out amongst the tangled tree limbs and dirt of their den.

It was fascinating.

A twig snapped behind him and Henri jolted his head to look, his heart rate quickening again. Just in time to see the white bob of her tail, he caught the sight of the doe leaping over the downed tree fifty feet behind him to his left as she disappeared into a thicket of shrubs.

Better a deer than a bear, he thought nervously and turned his gaze back towards the water.

That's why his mom was always telling him he couldn't come over to the river unless she or Poppy came along. Poppy always said bears were generally skittish but, if you met one, it was best to consider them unfriendly.

Living deep in the woods was a lot of fun and Henri never found himself bored or wondering what to do on a Saturday afternoon. But living this close to nature and its wildlife required a kid to be on his guard. Henri recognized that he was sharing this forest and this river, with wild animals like bear and wolves. And, they were animals, just doing what animals do.

After a few more minutes of patiently watching the den for movement but seeing none, and with an angry growl of hunger emanating from his stomach, Henri sat up in resignation and reached for his backpack.

This was not good. He didn't have much time left and he hadn't seen any movement down there at all. They were probably out searching for food.

Wanting to feel the sultry sun on his face, Henri shifted over to the edge of the rock cliff and hung his legs over the surface of the warm rock wall while he bit into his sandwich.

It really was cool living here, he thought. Much better than a house in town like some of his friends.

Henri loved the life – all the living things - that he found in the woods.

He loved the summers with the multitude of birds and critters living outside his back door. Sometimes, he'd wake up early, sit on the wide ledge of his bedroom window and watch the activity outside – like the stealthy slink of a mink hunting for a mouse or the skittish scurry of a rabbit. He'd say his prayers to God, thanking him again and again for this place and for Poppy coming to live with them.

Henri loved autumn with its layers of golds, oranges, reds and green, when the already-rich colors of the woods seemed to deepen even further. The air off Lake Superior would thin out and become crisp as the leaves in the woods crunched under your boot. Henri watched as small flocks of songbirds disappeared, on their annual search for warmer weather down south, and the critters dug in for the long winter.

With the arrival of winter, Henri found a whole set of new adventures outside. The thick blankets of fluffy snow allowed him to track all kinds of animals into the woods and along the banks of the frozen river, although given the depth in spots and it's steady current, you could never assume the river was frozen straight through.

But eventually, just as the long months of winter started to get on his nerves, the snow would begin to thaw, the river would appear from beneath its white blanket and begin to rush again with angry abandon. The animals would all come out of their winter hiding places and everything would start all over again.

Yes, Henri loved this life in the woods with his mom and with his grandpa Poppy. It was all a kid could ever dream of.

As he finished the last of his sandwich and was about to start on his apple, Henri watched with interest as a huge tree trunk snaked its way around the river's bend, raking huge sections of muck from the riverbank along with it. As it cleared the bend, it twisted and lodged upend amongst three big boulders that popped out of the river below Henri's feet.

Man! That tree trunk must be twelve feet long or better, Henri mused as he pulled back his legs cautiously. If the tree broke loose and fell his direction, not only would it crush the beaver den below him, but it could crash into the rock cliff and chop off his legs.

The white swirling water around its base worked ferociously against the stubborn tree and the slick surface of the boulders proved too slippery as the tree seemed to lose its grip and slid off again into the strong river current.

There it goes, Henri thought to himself as he watched the branches bounce off the rocks and under the water again. Off to the deep part down river, eventually floating towards the road where it would join the other large trees that hung up on the riverbank by the bridge around the bend.

Henri's eyes travelled the length of the river, watching as the tree rolled along the white swirling water. It caught on the riverbank about fifty yards downstream and then it floated away again, turning wildly in the water.

Just as he was losing sight of it around the next bend of the river, the tree stopped and stood ramrod straight again, dividing the rushing river on either side of it, its bedraggled branches shedding a shower of water and mud at the sudden change of momentum.

Henri stood up slowly to catch a better view, wondering what could have stopped the tree at that spot. The clearing on the riverbank with those aspen trees over there, where the grouse used to hatch, that was the edge of the deep part of the river. There weren't any boulders there, nothing impeded the river's current.

Curious, Henri squinted into his binoculars. Sunlight blinked across a metal object and bright slivers of light made him wince as they seemed to burn his eyes through the magnified lens. Adjusting his position slightly, he looked again.

The tree had shifted in the current and now it sat bouncing against the object, shielding it even more behind its branches, but Henri could still see sections of metal and what looked like a faded blue color.

Maybe it was a piece of sheet metal, he thought, *pulled off a building upriver?*

He continued to squint into the binoculars as he moved them along the shape of the object. *Was that a ... tire?*

Henri dropped the binoculars to his side and swallowed in disbelief, the juxtaposition of something so artificial was out of place in this untamed, natural environment.

Could it be a trailer? But how did it get here?

Or, maybe it was a car. And if it was a car, did that mean someone just ditched it in the river?

Or ... did that mean someone could be inside it?

Henri swallowed again and his heart rate quickened. He stuffed his snowshoes into his backpack and zipped it shut quickly, keeping his eyes on the distant, bouncing tree the whole time.

He would just have to go see what it was and then he would cut up to the bridge and walk home from that direction. It was the long way home, and it might make him late for the van that dropped Poppy off, but he wouldn't be home alone for very long by himself. It would be okay.

Henri trudged along the bank as quickly as the thick shrubbery and exposed tree roots would allow. The ground was uneven and slippery in spots and a few times, he slid precariously close to the rushing river.

By the time he reached the bend where the metal object still held the tree, his boots were caked with heavy mud and grass and his mittens were slippery with grime. The riverbank cut about ten feet above the water here and he couldn't see through the trees very well, so he stepped closer to the edge.

Pushing thorny branches away from his face and kicking some rocks out of his path, Henri tried to get a firm toe hold on the edge of the river bank as he stuck his head through the last veil of branches and examined the churning, noisy water below him.

It was a car all right. The left back tire and quarter panel poked above the water but the rest of it was lodged below, caught on something below the dark, swirling surface.

Henri squinted, focusing intently on seeing through the section of the back window that was still intact and visible. *Funny*, he thought. *It sure is strange that even with all the stuff hurling around in this river, that window isn't broken.*

But try as he might, he couldn't see anything through the grime and mud. In fact, now that he was close to it, the car didn't look shiny at all. It was dull and beaten up, parts of the exposed, once blue quarter panel were covered in a bright green slime and other parts were gray and weathered-looking.

Suddenly, over the rumbling noise of the river, he heard the shrill tone of a text notification bleeping on his cell phone in the pocket of his backpack.

His mom – or maybe it was Poppy back home now and wondering where he was. *Oh, boy. He must be super late!*

Pushing himself back from gnarled birch tree on the riverbank and hurrying through the woods towards the road, Henri swallowed hard over his guilty conscience for being at the river alone, exactly where he wasn't supposed to be. His mom would be mighty mad at him over this - she would probably ground him from his Xbox again - but this was well worth it. *Just think of the story he could tell Poppy! For sure, he would want to come back with him to check this out!*

As he trudged through the deep snow alongside the bridge on his way to the road, over his excitement, Henri labored hard in his mind about the car mystery. How did it get there and where was the person who drove it there?

Laughing nervously to himself, he thought about his initial feeling that someone might still be inside.

Me and my wild imagination – he reasoned with himself like his mother often did with him – *Just think about it, Henri. There wasn't a chance a person could be inside that car.*

From the looks of it, the river had laid claim to that car months ago, maybe even a year ago. It must have just emerged this spring because of the massive snow melt and the high waters that were ripping through the normally reserved riverbed.

Glancing back over his shoulder, imagining the tree bobbing alongside the half-buried car, Henri shook his head slowly and swallowed hard again.

No way. There was just no way a body could survive being buried in that river that long.

CHAPTER 2

April 2019

Drake

"Okay, I get it! I will talk to them, but you're making it a bigger deal than it is, Drake. The client *is* committed to Connor-Denning and they are pleased with the results overall. This is just a minor blip," Drake Connor's business partner Myles Denning frowned at him, concern furrowing his brow behind the heavy rimmed glasses he wore, "You *gotta lighten up*, man."

As he processed the admonition from his friend and partner, Drake Connor's silvery-blue eyes reflected the storm-darkened grays of the Chicago haze as he scanned the familiar view of the city skyline from his office window. Drawing his fingers through his short-cut, blonde hair and down his face, he smoothed his trim, dark brown beard in a reflexive movement, deep in thought.

The most recent programming tool had more than its fair share of bugs and it was dragging down other operating systems along with it. Never a good problem to find, especially so if the client was new.

With their IT security consulting business on fragile financial ground, they had to make good on every opportunity. There was no room for error on the client side. Revenues had to grow this year.

And, after the review he had just done of expenses, Drake was especially sensitive to hot spots on that side of the business too.

For example – the thought permeating his mind for the thousandth time – they were paying too much for rent in this building in this prestigious location. Was the business really able to leverage anything of value by officing at this spendy address?

Drake turned his eyes to regard Myles, but kept his thoughts to himself, as he was prone to do with this subject. If only his Chicago-born partner and his wife Emelie didn't live downtown, maybe they could consider moving their headquarters north where rents were more reasonable.

Moving his gaze beyond Myles's shoulder, Drake looked across his office to the windowed doors that opened out to the group of his thirty-plus employees. They all lived here too, they had families and lives tied to the inner suburbs and downtown.

He was the only one who had no family here; he was the only one who wanted out.

But, he reminded himself, this feeling was nothing new to him; it had been years now since he felt completely comfortable in his life. It didn't matter if it was the office location or a problem with a client, he was always quick to leap to the extreme and sometimes, the paranoid. It was something he was working on, this sense of all-or-nothing fatalism.

But who could really blame him? Fatalism was the by-product of that period of Drake's life when his wife divorced him for another man and then disappeared off the map altogether, leaving him the subject of a police investigation and with a cloud of scandal over his personal and professional life. At least that was his 30-second summary of it. And it wasn't something you included in your bio on Linked In.

For Drake, someone who was wired to take control of things, the loss of control was debilitating. As the days turned into months, the investigation became an all-consuming event that never left his consciousness.

Looking back on it now, years later, Drake attributed the upheaval surrounding Natalie's disappearance as the primary motivation for his deeper faith in God and his passion to live out his faith in his everyday life.

It also made him appreciate more fully those people who were loyal to him. His business partner Myles was one of those people. He had stood by him through the entire media-frenzied, traumatic ordeal as Drake and their business struggled back to life. Myles was a true friend and a guy who was comfortable enough to yank Drake out of self-imposed gloom if he saw it re-surface. Like now.

"You're right. Of course, you're right." Drake sighed deeply and walked to the rolling chair behind his desk, "I could go through the schematics with the team and help find the problem. It's probably a glitch in their operating system, something we just overlooked-"

As his voice rambled off, he loosened his tie and began to roll up the sleeves of his white dress shirt. It would be another long evening at the office for him, he thought as he drew his chair out from his desk and sat down, his eyes focused intently on his computer screens.

"Yeah, don't worry," Myles continued speaking as he walked towards the door, his smallish frame bouncing as he walked, "I told the client the response team is digging into it. On the upside, other than this blip, the beta test is going great. We've identified four compromised areas in their infrastructure already and we aren't even two weeks in."

"Oh, really?" Drake glanced up again, surprised at the good news, "I hadn't heard that. Wow, that's great!"

"Yes, it is. See what I mean?" Myles turned and grinned at the obvious relief written all over his partner's face, "Really, Drake, we're good at this. You're good at this. You gotta trust it, man. We are coming back with a vengeance."

"Couldn't have done it without you, Myles," Drake watched his partner's dark eyes crinkle as he smiled a self-deprecating grin, "No, seriously. You've gone above and beyond what a partner would be expected to. It means more to me than you know."

"Yeah, yeah, I know. And while I seriously enjoy your undying gratitude, you know that I'd expect the same from you," Myles laughed, "Besides, where else could I take a month-long sabbatical with my lovely wife and come back to such relative calm?"

Drake couldn't help smiling at his description of his excursion to Greece for his wedding and extended honeymoon in Emelie's home country where he met her large Greek family.

"Well, don't think I wasn't jealous when I had to leave, and you got to stay." Drake said dryly as he glanced at a text message that popped up from one of their sales directors in Minneapolis.

"If that's a love interest," Myles teased, noticing the text and backing towards the door again, "Go ahead and text her back. We're done here."

"Ah, no, nothing quite as exciting as that. It's Dan from Minneapolis. He was looking for approvals on expense reports and he also said the new hire is working out great and he's excited for us to meet her next week at the sales meeting."

"Oh, good!" Myles's expressive face beamed with enthusiasm, "Beth in Minneapolis and Juan here in Chicago, both solid hires. See? Things are looking up all around, Drake."

Focusing his gaze on Drake in mock sincerity, he continued, "Now might be a good time to focus on your personal life. I, for one, highly recommend marriage."

"Yeah - says the newlywed." Drake snorted as he hit the enter key on his keyboard, sending an approval for the expense reports that Dan needed.

"Well, sure, that's true," Myles admitted with a laugh, not quite ready to concede the point, "But the way you avoid relationships, one might be tempted to think you aren't over your ex."

"Ha, ha. Yeah, right. My ex-"

Just then, the office phone rang on his desk and the number on the display showed that it came directly to his phone instead of through the receptionist. Frowning slightly in confusion because Drake vaguely remembered the number that was displayed on caller-ID, he pushed the button for the speaker phone.

"Hello, Drake Connor here."

"Hey, Drake. This is Detective Miller. You remember me?"

"Uh, yes of course, Detective Miller. It's been quite a while."

Like three years, Drake thought over the lump in his throat as he frowned across the desk at his business partner whose face registered the surprise and confusion that Drake felt inside.

The ironic timing of it all. Here they were discussing Natalie, and out of the blue the detective who investigated her disappearance calls him on the phone. *Why was he calling now, after all this time?*

"Yes, it has been quite a while, Drake. I have some news that might interest you and I wanted you to hear it from me before it hits the media."

"Okay. And that is-"

"We've found your ex-wife, Drake. We've found Natalie."

CHAPTER 3

1992-1996

Natalie

It's not like I planned for my life to go this way. I didn't expect to end up on the run. Not like this - here in this car, hidden deep in these woods.

At one time, I could have passed for normal. I had a mom and a dad. We moved from Atlanta to live in a nice house in Edina, Minnesota. We even had a swimming pool in the back yard.

Then, my dad died from cancer.

My mom lost the house and the swimming pool.

I was ten.

My mom was pretty, and soft-spoken in a decorous, southern-belle kind of way. It didn't take her long to meet Him. It took her even less time to marry him because he had a nicer house and a bigger swimming pool. She said I should like my new stepfather, call him Dad.

I hated him. I hated everything about him. The way he talked, the way he moved, the way he smelled. I hated the way he brushed against me when she was out of the room, I hated the way he breathed his whiskey breath into my ear at night and the way he would pinch me and then tell me not to cry or he would do even worse to my mother. I hated his hands and his fists and the bruises I had to hide.

Four years went by.

Four years is a long time. It's an eternity to a kid.

A kid can come up with lots of plans in four years – I called them fantasies. When the weather was nice, I'd sit on a flat part of our shingled roof, three stories up, just outside my bedroom window and I'd plan my "other" life.

In my other life, I was away from that house. Far, far away. Away from him.

It happened when I was fourteen.

I was being so quiet up there on my roof that dark, dark night. I'd been up there so often that spring and he'd never found me. I didn't think he even knew about my hiding spot.

I thought I was safe there.

But I was fourteen and what did I know? I was wrong. He knew exactly where to find me.

It was his fault, not mine. I don't remember pushing him.

I just remember his black eyes and his smelly breath. I remember his laugh as he reached out for my ankle and I shimmied away, trying to kick at him. I remember his fingers pulling at my legs, he was pinching me, telling me what he wanted to do to me and laughing at me.

And, then he was gone.

The night swallowed up his laugh.

I waited, too scared to look over the eave, now broken and dangling, to see where he had landed. I watched our neighbor's house for any sudden movement, wondering if anyone saw him fall. But nothing happened, no one noticed.

I waited for a while longer.

Finally, I inched to the edge of the roof and looked down, but I couldn't see the ground very well through the trees and the shrubs alongside the house.

I watched as two kids on their bikes rode past on the street in front of our house. I squinted to see them under the streetlight. They never even glanced my way.

Eventually, I crawled off the roof and tip-toed downstairs, thinking he must be back inside the house, tending to his wounds and swearing a blue streak about what he'd do to me now.

As I rounded the corner to the kitchen, I couldn't breathe, and my ribs ached in a kind of premonition of the punches that I knew would come.

But the house was silent.

My head started to swim with the sound of my pounding heartbeat in my ears and I looked with dread at the screen door that led to the back yard. I watched as my shaking hand opened the screen door and then jumped as it snapped shut behind me.

The backyard was full of long shadows that fanned away from the single light above the back door. Creeping alongside the house, I peeked around the corner, searching the shadows on the ground below my hiding spot on the roof three stories above.

There he was.

He was lying face-up on the patio, no more than three feet away from me, half hidden by a shrub.

His eyes were lifeless.

I didn't want to look but I was drawn to his face, trying to prove to myself that it was real. And when I looked, I found nothing but a lifeless stare, eyes so vacant that they looked hollow straight through.

That's when I knew I was toast, that my life was forever changed.

Is it wrong that I only thought of myself in that moment? Do you judge me for it? Because that's what I did - I thought of my fourteen-year-old self. I sure didn't think about him or that he had breathed his last, hateful breath.

No, I didn't think about him for even a split second.

Later, I would realize that my lack of feeling was an indication of how dark I am inside. A sociopath – someone who feels no sense of pain, no empathy for others' pain.

But, if I am a sociopath, then I join an army of them. I've met many in my lifetime. And my stepfather was the supreme leader of us all.

Now, I see that the moment he left this earth will never leave me. I've been stained with it. It's left me the inkiest black of the darkest night sky - that's my soul.

There have been moments in my life where I wonder if I can fix the picture of who I am. More than once, I've tried to erase the charcoal lines, to lighten them enough to see my color again. But these attempts have been half-hearted and futile. Something - or someone - always reminds me of who I am.

And, after these failed attempts to be normal, all I'm left with are dirty, smudged fingers and a residue that reminds me that I will never be clean again.

I didn't even go back into the house that night. I didn't call my mom at the country club and I didn't call 911. Instead, I snuck into the garage, got on my bike and rode away, my plan taking shape in my mind as each block passed behind me.

I would just pretend like I wasn't even at the house that night and I knew right away who I would ask to help me with my plan.

When I got to his house, he listened while I told him the whole story. I didn't shed a tear when I told him. Not one tear.

TC was like me - his soul was rotten black like mine.

Even though he was three years older than me, I knew it the first time I met him that he and I were the same. It didn't matter that I lived in a nice house on a respectable street and he lived with a foster family in a shack on a street lined with run-down shacks - we both were damaged.

That night, TC was home alone. No one saw me arrive.

So, together, we came up with the story. It had just enough details that it sounded plausible but not so many that we might mess up as we re-told the lie: I went over to his house straight after track practice and was with him all night, playing video games.

TC worked it all out and told me he would be my alibi if anyone – as in, the cops - ever asked.

He was used to lying, he said.

It was easy, he said.

If you really, really wanted the lie to be the truth, it was easy to lie.

CHAPTER 4

April 2019

Sella & Henri

"–well, poor thing. I don't know what I'd have done, finding a – dead body – like that." Marianne, owner of The Hair Hut, one of three hair salons in Twin Shores, clucked under her breath and slid a sympathetic glance towards Henri who sat in a plastic chair impatiently waiting for his mother's haircut to finish.

"Yes, it was an eventful day, that's for sure." Sella said as noncommittally as possible, not wanting to encourage any further gossip than was already lighting up the small town. Besides, she had to get Henri over to the sheriff's department for some further questioning. She sure didn't have time to trash over Henri's discovery with Marianne and her excitement-starved customers.

"But do you know who she was?" Marianne pursued the topic with open interest, not catching Sella's clue, "You know, everyone is talking about it 'round here."

"Well, sorry, I have nothing to report." To change the subject, and noticing that Marianne was reaching for her large-barrel curling iron, Sella cleared her throat and asked accusingly, "What do you think you're going to do with that?"

"Oh! I just thought we could try giving you a little extra bounce today." Marianne set the curling iron down, flipped her fine-tooth metal comb between her fingers and puffed up the back of Sella's hair.

Glancing at the result of her work, Marianne pursed her mouth and raised her perfectly arched eyebrows in a doubtful expression as she regarded Sella in the mirror above the bottle-laden hair station.

If Marianne had the guts to say what she's really thinking, Sella thought to herself as she grimaced at her own reflection in the mirror, *she'd tell me that a healthy dose of makeup and some eye liner wouldn't hurt either because thirty-four years is looking a little tough on you today, Sella.*

These early days of spring, after surviving a brutal winter like they'd just had, Sella's fair complexion was left devoid of any color and her brown eyes looked extra mousy and dull. On the positive side, Sella did consider it her good fortune that she had inherited her mother's dark eyelashes and eyebrows so that made it easier for her to ignore the meager assortment of make-up on her bathroom counter each morning, choosing instead to go simple and unadorned.

Besides, the guys at work would undoubtedly notice if she suddenly showed up wearing make-up and a new hair style. Any attempt by her at self-improvement would be met with comments along the line of - 'What, Sella, you goin' to a wedding or somethin?'

Definitely not worth it.

"No, Marianne, just leave it, I'm good. Besides, I'm about the least bouncy person you know." Sella smiled thinly, combed her fingers through her hair and tucked a few wayward strands behind her ear, curling them back into their comfortable place. Succumbing many years ago to the natural wave of her hair, Sella now embraced the convenience of it and the hairstyle she'd worn for over five years suited her just fine.

"Of course. Whatever you want, Sella. The customer is always right." Marianne muttered through a forced smile as she replaced the unused curling iron between two bottles of hair spray.

"I gotta head back to the store later anyway and I don't have anyone to impress over there. At least not today." Sella quipped as she removed the plastic cape from around her shoulders and reached into her front pocket for some money. Judging by Marianne's blank expression, she noticed her dry joke fell flat.

"Gotcha, no problem," Marianne glanced across the hair salon at the two other stylists who were engaged in conversations with their respective clients, "You know, me and the girls were talkin' about that just the other day. We said we couldn't imagine how you do it, working with all those men at that auto shop. All day, *every day*. We gotta hand it to ya', Sella, you must have real thick skin. It would drive me insane if I had to work with my brothers every day!"

Noting that her life seemed a peculiar form of torture to them and completely befuddled that any aspect of her life would be interesting fodder for The Hair Hut stylists, Sella shrugged and responded, "Yeah, well, I guess I'm used to it. You learn to live with it."

With a tight smile and wave goodbye to the other two stylists, Sella crossed the salon and placed the payment for her haircut under the stapler that sat on the counter by the door and took Henri's hand as he joined her with a relieved grin.

Glad that she wouldn't need a haircut for another six weeks, Sella stepped out into the bright, north-shore Minnesota afternoon and breathed in the lake breeze, with its happy mix of slightly earthy, yet fresh, watery fragrance.

Given its location, perched high on a ridge of the Lake Superior shoreline, springtime in Twin Shores always seemed to arrive in a tantalizing ebb and flow of promisingly warm, sunlit days followed by a series of drizzly days where the air turned brisk off the lake as it bit through your jacket and made your eyes water.

Today was one of the warm days, with the promise of spring in the light breeze.

Stepping gingerly over the steady flow of snow melt that trailed alongside the curbing next to her parked Jeep, Sella scaled the distance from the curb into the driver's seat while her son joined her in the seat next to her.

"Your hair looks nice, Mom." Henri said, in his innocent, 10-year-old way as he pulled his door closed and pushed his longish, dark curls out of his eyes.

"Ah, thanks, bud. And thanks for hanging in there waiting for me. Let's go see what else the sheriff needs to talk to us about, ok?"

"-we appreciate your willingness to bring Henri in to answer a few more questions, Sella. I know the past couple of days have been kinda crazy. We just need to finish up some statements for our paperwork." Sheriff Cooper handed Sella a cup of coffee and smiled at Henri as he handed him the can of root beer and sat down across the table from them.

"Thank you, sir," Henri said formally and pulled back the tab to take a long drink. Root beer was his favorite and something his mom never bought at the grocery store. Too much sugar, she said.

Henri knew Sheriff Cooper, so he wasn't very intimidating even though he wore a gun in his side holster. They went to the same church and often the sheriff would join his wife Val when she taught Sunday school. Sometimes he wore his sheriff's uniform to church, sometimes he didn't.

Today he was wearing his uniform. They were sitting at the sheriff's station in a room with maps on the walls and a window that looked out over the dispatch area with the chirping radios and the two ladies who worked there. It seemed kind of quiet, considering that two days ago they had found a dead body in the river a few miles away.

"So, Henri," Sheriff Cooper focused his steady gaze on him, "I know it's probably a little scary that we found a woman in that car and I'm sure her family will want us to give them as much information as possible. Let's go over some of the things you told me Wednesday evening. Was that the first time you noticed the car?"

Henri glanced in hesitation at his mom and swallowed hard over his slurp of root beer. He was still in trouble for going to the river alone. He didn't really like to talk about it because his mom got that mad look on her face, her lips would clamp together into a hard line and her eyes turned a dangerous, dark color.

She said that the look on her face was Concern, not Mad. But Henri thought it looked a lot like Mad. Most of the time his mom was really nice, until she got "concerned."

"Uh huh, that was the first time I noticed it." He smoothed down his unruly hair and nodded. He thought it was best to say as little as possible, that way he would get in less trouble.

"Okay. You said you had also been at the river in the days before Wednesday too. Had you been at the spot in the river where we found the car on those other days? Do you think you might have missed it?"

"Nu-uh," Henri shook his head side to side. He was sure he would have seen that car if it had been there those other days.

But - he wondered desperately - why did the sheriff have to remind his mom that he had been to that river lots of times? *This was making it so much worse.* Henri glanced down at the root beer can in his hand to avoid looking at his mom.

"Okay," Sheriff Cooper wrote something on the sheet of paper in front of him and then continued, "The water is really high this year and you said that there was a lot of stuff floating around in the river like rocks and tree branches. Did you see anything floating around that didn't belong there? Like any personal items or clothing? Anything like that?"

"No, I didn't. Sir." Henri hesitated expectantly, wanting to answer the sheriff's questions in the most adult way he could. When the sheriff smiled at him, he took another swallow of root beer with a sigh of relief.

This wasn't so bad, Henri thought, relieved at how it was going. His mom didn't look super mad at him and now she was even smiling a little. So, Henri continued more confidently, "I just saw the tire through my binoculars and then went to check it out."

"Did you try to look in the car? Maybe try to open a door or anything?"

"No, it was too far away. I couldn't see anything, that's why I asked Poppy to come back with me to look at it better."

"And did your grandfather get to the car? I ask this because you know your grandpa had a hard time remembering much when he talked to us."

"Yeah, you know - he has troubles with his memory. When we got back there, he was able to see better because that tree had moved and got crammed in between the shoreline and the car."

"So, he crawled out onto the tree and could see inside?"

"Yeah-" Henri stopped, the memory giving him a shiver under his hoodie. The look on Poppy's face was really spooky – almost like he'd seen a ghost. Henri shivered again and looked up at the sheriff.

"I know it's kind of scary, Henri. But we need to help that lady's family figure this out," Sheriff Cooper leaned forward slightly, his eyes focused on Henri's. "We think this lady's car has been in the river for a long time, so she's been – gone – for quite a while. But this is really important, Henri. Did your grandpa reach into the car or touch anything in the car? Like the lady's purse or anything like that?"

"No, he just looked down into the car and told me that there was a dead lady in there because he could see her hair." At this statement, Henri could see his mom frown, it must have been the way he said it.

"Okay. And, that's when your grandfather called 911?"

"Yes, but he had me talk to the 911 lady when he got her on the phone. He was too nervous, he said I'd better do it."

"Yes, Doris the 911 operator told me that. You did a great job. You gave good directions so we could find you." Sheriff Cooper sat back in his chair and sighed heavily, "Well, I guess that's it then. Thanks." He wrote something else on the sheet of paper before raising his eyes again.

"Say, Henri," He asked, "Can I talk to your mom alone for a moment? You can go out and listen to the radios for a while if you want. Might be some interesting stuff going on."

"Sure, thanks." Taking his root beer with him, Henri left the room and closed the door behind him, glad that his interrogation was over, and it wasn't even that bad. Although he'd never tell Sheriff Cooper this, his mom was a lot scarier than him and she never carried a gun on her hip.

Sheriff Cooper was better known as "Coop" to Sella. He had always just been Coop. The best friend of her oldest brother Phillip, as a boy Duane Cooper had a job at her dad's shop after school to earn some extra spending money.

Mostly though, Coop found himself getting in the way of the more experienced mechanics. Often, when Luca reviewed Coop's work on an engine, he would replace the wrench in Coop's hand with a broom and tell him to sweep the shop. Everyone – especially the customers and Luca's business reputation - had been much better off for it.

Now, turning his gaze from Henri as he left the room, Sheriff Cooper smiled easily at her and said, "You're doing a great job with him, Sella. I know it's tough for you living out there alone-with Henri, and your dad. Well, I know it's a lot." Coop shrugged and crossed his legs casually in front of him.

"We're doing okay, Coop. Thanks, though." Sella smiled tightly at the tone in his voice. She was sure from his expression that she had been the topic of conversation again between Coop and her well-meaning, but slightly over-protective, brother.

"Yeah, I know, but-" He paused uncomfortably with a slight grin, as if he knew he shouldn't say more but their history somehow required it from him, "You seeing anyone yet, Sella? It's going on three years now since the divorce, isn't it?"

"Yes, it is. And, no I'm not." She said the words firmly, enunciating each syllable, as if by some miracle her tone of voice could stop him from proceeding to tell her she'd better hurry up and "find a guy."

"Well, don't get prickly about it now, Sella. I'm not trying to be nosy," His smile was boyish and familiar, "You never know - maybe I'm asking for someone."

"Yes, this isn't news to me, Coop," Sella interrupted, "Phillip told me about the new deputy that moved up from Duluth. Do you two really have nothing better to do with your time than play match-makers?"

"Ha, ha," He squinted with surprise at her comment and leaned back casually, "Well, maybe I like the guy and I want to make sure he makes this town his forever-home. Finding a match would be a good start. You know, you could try to help me out here - it's not easy to find good help nowadays."

"Yeah, well, please look somewhere else, would you?" Sella straightened in her chair and met his eyes seriously, "Now. I know your deputy's love life wasn't the reason you asked us back here today."

Coop smiled at her hard turn in the conversation and took a deep breath before leaning forward and continuing, "No, you're right. There were just some things that I needed to clear up from your dad's and Henri's statements the other day."

"Yes, you can see – well, can you tell how much worse the Alzheimer's has gotten?" Although Coop knew her father, Luca, they didn't cross paths often anymore, so Sella wasn't sure how much Coop knew about her father's illness.

"Yeah, it sure was sad. But, finding something like this is bound to be a shock for anyone. No one blames him for being confused."

"I still can't believe that he climbed out onto that tree like that, so close to that dangerous water. I'm not sure who makes me angrier, Henri or Dad," Sella huffed then leaned closer towards him intently, trying to calm herself down, "I wasn't there the whole time you were talking to Dad. What did he say that's confusing to you?"

"Oh, I don't think it's anything important," Sheriff Cooper said, "Just something he maybe thought he saw, but who knows? He mentioned a lady's purse, he called it a pocketbook. He said he had it, but when I asked where it was, he couldn't remember where he put it."

"And, Henri said that he never saw Dad find a purse–" Sella mused, her brow knit in confusion.

36

"Exactly. So, I think Luca might just be making that part up in his mind. But just keep your eyes open for anything like that. Bring it in if you find it."

"But, still, somehow – you figured out who the lady is?"

"Yeah, the car came up previously registered in Chicago and we found three different passports, two were fakes, one of them was real," Coop sat back in his chair and rubbed the stubble on his chin thoughtfully, "It's got us thinking, that's for sure. Course it wouldn't be the first time someone came up here to these woods trying to get lost. It happens all the time."

"I suppose," Sella nodded, deep in thought. She could relate to that sentiment. *Lots of times she just wanted to get lost in these woods.*

"A person thinks you know everyone in this small town, but do you, really?" Coop said quietly, closed his notebook and set his pen carefully across it, "Sella, you didn't know a woman named Natalie Sartell, did you?"

"No, I didn't. Was she from around here?"

"She wasn't listed as a missing person in the state of Minnesota and she didn't live around here, from what we can tell. Her address is listed as Chicago. Best we can figure, it appears she was headed for Canada."

"Yeah," Sella nodded, thinking of the conversation she overheard between her brother and some local busybodies at the shop yesterday, "I heard you found some money in that cooler that was in the car with her. Running to Canada would make sense, wouldn't it?"

"Yeah. It will be out in the media soon, so I guess it's no secret. We found a lot of money and some jewelry in the car with her, so another agency is involved in tracking all that down. Sounds like she stole a bunch of money from her husband's business in Chicago back in 2015."

The year hit Sella like a thud. Without even realizing it, the years clicked back like a calendar in Sella's mind to a happier time for her and for Henri.

2015. A year when she was still married, and Henri still had a father.

Pushing the thoughts of her past life out of her mind, Sella focused on Coop again and the uncomfortable reminder of the dead woman in the submerged car.

"So, you think she's been – in the river – for four years?" The thought made Sella squeamish. All that time, within a mile of their house.

"Best we can tell by the – state of decomposition - yes."

"Wow, that's creepy. But I don't get it. How did she end up in the river?"

"Hard to say, probably an accident. But we're still looking into it and you understand- I can't say anything else on it right now."

"Sure. Well, I don't know if we can help with anything else but let us know. And, if I find a purse or if Dad remembers anything else, I'll let you know." Sella moved in her chair and rose from her chair.

"Thanks, Sella," Sheriff Cooper crossed the small room and held the door open for her, easily slipping back into the annoying 'older brother' mode, and taunted her as she passed him, "And, his name is Zach, by the way. Deputy Zachary Wyler."

"Who-" Sella stopped, momentarily confused and then mock-punched him on the arm when she saw his grin, "Okay, Sheriff, that's enough. I think you should just stick to law enforcement. Your match-making skills leave a lot to be desired."

CHAPTER 5

May 2019

Drake

Detective Miller, a stout man with thick arms wrapped in hair like a bristle brush, stood with his arms crossed and resting on his round stomach as he gazed out the window of Drake's apartment towards the choppy waters of Lake Michigan two blocks away.

The man hadn't changed much in three years, Drake thought as he pushed the button on his coffee maker. Although the years had peppered his wiry, cinnamon-colored hair with silver-gray and the wrinkles on his forehead and around his mouth had deepened considerably, Detective Miller looked pretty much the same as the last time Drake had seen him - the day three years ago when he'd finally been cleared as a suspect in Natalie's disappearance.

"-so we have been piecing things together, Drake," The detective continued as he turned away from the window, "but I have to say we still have a lot of holes in this investigation and we hope you can help us out with some of them."

His slightly cynical, inquisitive manner sure hadn't changed, Drake noticed dryly as he remembered the many meetings they'd had. But these characteristics were probably the unavoidable consequence of too many missing person investigations and most of them with "holes in them."

"Well, honestly Detective, I'm still trying to process the fact that Natalie isn't missing but instead she's - dead." Drake finished the comment with a croak.

He pulled the full cup from the coffee maker and walked around the counter towards the couch as he continued, trying to put his jumbled thoughts in order, "I had no idea where she'd gone, but to find out that she's- dead. Well, that's been a shock."

Drake set the cup on a coaster, sat down in the leather club chair, and waited for the detective to join him, hoping he'd share more about what they'd learned in the investigation. Maybe Detective Miller could help him come to terms with the fact that the woman he'd once loved had died years ago and he never knew it.

For the past three days, since taking the phone call, Drake had been walking around in a stupor. The emotions that he thought he had put behind him six plus years ago when Natalie left him – love, sorrow, loss – they all came flooding back with the telephone call the other day.

That had always been his trouble when it came to Natalie. He loved her, he believed her, he trusted her - but he'd never really known her at all.

"So, remind me, Drake. How long were you married to Natalie Sartell?" Detective Miller eased himself into a chair, straightening his tie over his stomach as he did so.

"About a year and a half." Drake replied.

It still hurt to hear her referred to as Natalie Sartell – the name of the other guy - instead of Natalie Connor. It had been years since she was called Natalie Connor. *Why was it so hard for him to get over it?*

"And, she started working as an accountant for Rolph Sartell at his construction company during the time you were married?"

"Yes," Drake took a slow swallow of his coffee to try to compose himself before answering, "She started in the fall of 2013."

"So, she starts working for Rolph Sartell as his accountant, learns his business inside out and at some point, she became involved in an affair with him?" Detective Miller's tone was matter of fact; not necessarily cruel, but he sure wasn't trying to handle the demise of Drake's marriage delicately either.

"Yes," Drake managed to utter, finding it difficult not to let the bitterness ooze out every syllable, "Eventually, I found out about the affair and although I wanted to try to work on our marriage, it didn't take long and she left me for him."

"Remind me when that was, could ya, Drake?" Detective Miller raised his cup to his mouth and waited for the answer with bushy brown eyebrows raised.

"Our divorce?" Drake asked, wondering painfully why he had to go through all this again with this guy and when all this would finally stop, "We signed papers the end of January 2014."

"So, eventually she marries the other guy, and less than six months after the wedding, she steals his money and hightails off for Canada. All by herself?" Detective Miller scowled in disbelief at the scenario and his eyes pinned Drake to the wall with their hard glint. This line of questioning was making Drake feel as if, somehow, he was in the crosshairs of the investigation again. Maybe they thought he was her accomplice or something.

"Well," Drake continued, trying to keep his voice even and controlled, "I know she married him, and *you* told me that she stole money from him. Then I heard it all over the news. I never knew anything about any of that," Drake shifted in his chair under the detective's uncomfortable stare, "Truth was, I rarely spoke to Natalie after they married. Maybe a couple of times to pass off personal items that she left at the apartment, but that was all. When it – our marriage I mean – when it was over for her, it was really over."

"So, do you think she somehow 'marked' the guy?"

"As in– ?"

"As in she 'played' him for his money," If it was possible, the stare in Detective Miller's brown eyes hardened even further as he questioned, "Was that the type of woman your ex was, Drake?"

"Well, I don't–" *Go ahead, Drake,* he told himself, *be honest. You have thought this very same thought many times over the years.*

"Now would be the opportunity to tell me, Drake - did Natalie steal anything from you?"

You mean anything other than my heart and soul?

Drake dropped his head to stare at the tops of his shoes, trying to form the words of an appropriate response in his mind.

"No, she didn't steal any money from me, Detective Miller," No one needed to know the true extent of the damage that his ex-wife had done to him so Drake continued with as honest an answer as he could muster, "Although I have wondered over the years if she meant to. And, if she did want to steal from me, I have no idea what stopped her."

"Yes, well, you seem to be a likely target, business owner and all," Detective Miller stated flatly before he sighed and continued, "Maybe she planned to shake you down, but a bigger fish swam into the pond before she got around to it. And wasn't it just her luck that Rolph Sartell had his own skeletons he was trying to hide so who knows how tightly she wound the noose before she bolted."

"Yeah, I guess," Drake mumbled, but he wasn't thinking about Natalie's theft right now, or her ultimate fate. Instead, he was lost in the memory of the warm June afternoon they were married. Natalie's soft, blonde hair was lifting in the breeze and catching on her long eyelashes as they walked out of the church to the greet the small group of guests on the sidewalk outside. Her infectious laugh that somehow carried the lilt of a soft southern accent, his heart thumping inside his chest at the treasure he'd found and now could call his wife–

"–I guess we should be grateful for the attention her 'little caper' brought to Rolph Sartell's organization," Detective Miller continued after a sip of his coffee, "Without the notoriety, it might have been years before law enforcement figured out what he was up to and put him in prison."

"I guess I only know what I read in the news at the time. But it doesn't surprise me that Natalie caught on right away to his construction fraud and tax evasion. She always was good with numbers."

"Yeah, and she used that asset – and a few of her other assets – to her advantage with him, didn't she?"

Drake couldn't help but be shocked at the comment and the insinuation behind it. It was true, however. Natalie was a beautiful, intelligent woman and she'd never known a man she couldn't influence with that beauty and intelligence; it was part of her charm.

At first when Natalie went missing four years ago, she was considered the victim, above reproach. Gradually, it was discovered that she had been stealing from her husband's company and her disappearance began to look like a cover-up or worse, a potential homicide. Both Drake and Rolph Sartell had been suspects in her disappearance.

Now, with the discovery of her dead body, apparently through a car accident, and the stolen cash found along with her, there were even more questions.

With each discovery, Natalie moved ever further away from victim and ever closer to perpetrator.

"Yeah, I guess she did use her assets to get what she wanted." Drake summarized his thoughts sadly.

"Well, be that as it may, I came to tell you, the missing person's case is closed. I do this as a courtesy to you, Drake." Detective Miller sat forward in his chair and leaned his elbows on his knees.

"Okay, thank you. I appreciate that-"

"But I want to ask you something before I go. Consider it a personal favor." The detective's voice took on a familiar, go-along-to-get-along tone.

"Okay-" Drake hesitated, not sure what he could do to help a detective.

"You told me a few years ago that you still loved your ex-wife, even after she left you for another guy, and that's stuck with me. Now that we know she was a thief and she's now deceased I wonder if you have as many questions as I do about where she was headed with all that cash – and with whom."

"Sure, I have questions. But aren't the police the ones who find those answers, Detective?"

"Of course. And they are still on this one, believe me. But, with Rolph Sartell in prison and no record of this cash ever being reported as stolen, I was thinking we might need to be 'creative' in our attempt to figure out the plan she was working at the time of her accident."

"And how can I help with that?"

"Just ask around about her, you know, her family, friends. You said at the time of her disappearance that you were relatively close to some of her family, right?"

"Well, up until the divorce I was. But when she married Sartell, those relationships kind of dropped off."

"Okay, but still it wouldn't be completely off-base for you to connect with a few of those people, would it? You know, as a way to 'deal with her passing' kind of thing. Who knows? Maybe she contacted one of them during her escape."

It might be possible that Natalie's family would talk to him, Drake thought. But then the memories of the early days of the investigation roared back to him and the texts from Natalie's mom with the accusations that her family was sure he must be involved in Natalie's disappearance flicked through his mind.

If her family could believe that of him then, what would have changed their mind by now? Would he really want to open himself up to all of that again? He had re-started his life. What good would it do to open up old wounds?

"Oh, boy," Drake spoke his hesitation without realizing it, "I don't know, Detective. I'm not sure I want to get involved-"

The detective squinted as if surprised and a bit disappointed. The expression on his hard face looked as if he just realized that Drake wasn't quite the man he had expected him to be.

"Of course, Drake," His words through his deep sigh were conciliatory, but his tone was not, "No, you're right. Natalie *Sartell* died under a cloud of mystery, not Natalie *Connor*. I don't know what I was thinking. It's just the detective in me that would think you might want to know about her last movements. Sorry 'bout that. You're right to feel 'uninvolved'. Forget I said anything."

As he waved his hands to finish the thought, Detective Miller rose from the chair and started walking across the room.

"Okay, yeah. I don't think I could be of any help anyway," Drake followed him to the door, somehow feeling like he let the detective and himself down, "But I do hope they get to the bottom of it. There are still a lot of unanswered questions."

"Yes, there are. But, unfortunately, that's just another day at the office for us," Detective Miller turned slightly and smiled a half-smile, more like a grimace, "See ya 'round, Drake. Take care of yourself."

CHAPTER 6

1996-1997

Natalie

I notice things about people, that's one of my strengths. I watch how they act and react. It helps me figure them out. You never know when a strength like that might be useful.

For instance, I noticed the morning of my stepfather's funeral that my mom spent an extra hour primping in front of her mirrored vanity. She wore a new shade of Avon lipstick called Scarlet Summer and she twisted and pinned her lush blonde hair up at the back of her head with hair clips that sparkled with cubic zirconia. This hair style, one that I'd never seen her wear before that day, allowed the most flattering view of her simple, diamond stud earrings and her graceful, flawless neck.

My mother floated around the house that morning, wavering between hand wringing as she practiced her grieving widow act and nervous energy wondering aloud who would show up to the funeral. Certainly, the entire country club would feel obligated to show their respects, wouldn't they? She asked me. As if I would know or care.

It was obvious that on a basic, instinctual level my mom was already on the hunt for my next stepfather. I say this without malice. Well, not too much anyway.

My mom was a pragmatist. Although she controlled and manipulated men in her own way, she also needed them for financial security and emotional security. I could see that. It was something I noticed.

The fact that my mom needed a man was something that I hated about her. Not that I hated my mother as a person, I really did love her in lots of ways, I just saw through her and some of what I saw, I really hated.

Weakness. I saw weakness in her financial dependence on men. But I must admit, I really respected her willingness to use men. She didn't think twice about using men to get what she needed.

You might be wondering, did my mom freak out when she found my stepfather dead in the back yard? The answer is Yes ... and No.

Because my mom was a pragmatist, she overcame the initial shock and seemed to move on, never really questioning why something so strange would happen to him.

She theorized that he must have been working on the roof and simply lost his footing, falling to his death. It didn't seem to bother her that she had never seen him on the roof before. It was obvious from the way she spoke that she didn't know about my hiding spot and never considered that I could be involved.

The day after it happened, I stood in the back of the room while the cops sat down at our kitchen table with my mother and interviewed her. As she spoke, her blue-violet eyes welled up with tears, and she asked the cops for a tissue. When one of them dutifully went to the bathroom and came back with a box, she smiled and drawled softly, "Thanks, hon."

That's about all it took. Her story became truth.

No one asked any further questions and the coroner ruled it an accident. The life insurance money that arrived a few months later was safely deposited into the bank, to be used sparingly until she secured my next stepfather.

All through it, I said nothing.

My mother had no clue. She believed me when I said I hadn't been at home that night. She believed my lie and it became hers.

I learned that TC was right. It was easy to lie if you really, really wanted the lie to be the truth.

I began to see that TC was right about a lot of things. TC, by the way, is short for Tony Carmine.

I was captivated by him. He had a full-blooded-Italian-in-a-Scandinavian-world exotic look with dark, tousled hair and gorgeous, expressive features. He didn't look like the boy next door, he looked like trouble.

At first, we were "just" friends. Of course, I was infatuated with him immediately and eventually we became more than just friends, but not at first. We shared secrets as friends, without the need to lie to each other.

Now I see that's why I trusted TC - even though I witnessed his lies to others daily - to me, he didn't lie.

It was an understanding between us.

When I shared with him the depth of my dark heart that night - the degree to which I had no remorse for another person's life or death - we figured out that we were the same.

The September after my stepfather died, TC started his senior year in high school. He was taking college-level computer programming classes in high school even before that kind of thing was commonplace, but ironically, TC absolutely hated school.

He said school was for followers, people that had no imagination. He told me that he had resigned himself to high school and college because to "work the circles of money and influence out there," one had to sacrifice a few brain cells and get a degree.

My grades were just barely above average, and I preferred to sit at the back of the class and fade into the bulletin boards that no one ever looked at. I told TC that I didn't mind being a "follower" because I liked to disappear.

Don't get me wrong, it's not like I wanted to follow someone else's direction. No. Absolutely, quite the opposite.

I sat dutifully in class because I wanted to see how easily I could make them think I was following, while at the same time, I broke every rule possible.

I cheated on tests, even when I knew the information. I forged my mom's handwriting on notes to stay home sick, even when she would have written them for me. I stole money from her, even when she would have gladly given it to me if I had asked.

It was the thrill of deception - of appearing one way to the world while being another – that's what thrilled me.

So, when I say that TC and I were the same, what I mean is that our methods were different, but we had similar goals. And we weren't slowed by a moral conscience. We understood the extent to which we were different than most kids.

We skipped school together and eventually started lifting stuff from convenience stores around the city. Nothing high dollar, just cigarettes, snacks and Schmidt beer. TC always came up with the plan, he called me his accomplice.

He showed me how he was stealing money through credit card scams and how he was hacking into people's computers, stealing their personal data and selling it to other scammers. It was all very techy and exciting.

The year I spent with him before he went to college was the best year of my life. Each month built on the one before and by the end of that year, I felt like we would be together always, living off our wits, making money off those less fortunate. TC would always have a plan.

Then, in September, he left Minnesota to attend university in Phoenix, Arizona and I was left alone to my meager high school existence with very few girls that I could call friends and all the "boys next door."

Life without him? It was a life without color.

CHAPTER 7

August 2019

Drake

Through the glass doors, Drake noticed that the office had grown quiet and Rene, the receptionist, had turned off the lights behind her desk. As she finished tying the laces on her running shoes, she stood up and grinned a "see you Monday" smile and pulled the gym bag string tight over the heels she had stored inside. She was the last of the staff to leave that Friday afternoon, many of her co-workers had ducked out before 4:00 pm. It was a shimmering, summer Friday afternoon after all and most people had a life.

Drake smiled at Rene in acknowledgment and returned his attention to the phone call with his Minneapolis client. They were wrapping up the details on the programming package that he planned to present to them in a week. Just a few minor tweaks on it over the next couple of days and the program would be exactly what they were looking for. As he closed out the call, Drake felt more confident than ever, that the meeting next week would be the first step in a successful long-term relationship.

After making some notes for the design team, Drake pulled the client plans together into a neat stack and slid them into the blue and white Conner-Denning Security file folder. As he sat back in his chair with a sigh, his eyes travelled the length of his desk, landing once again on the client file folder. AGRITECH IP, WOODBURY, MN

Woodbury, Minnesota. A suburb just across the Mississippi River from the Minneapolis/St. Paul airport. Home to this agricultural business client and home to his ex-parents-in-law Allison and Don.

The thought that had been convicting him since this business meeting was arranged two weeks ago flashed again through his mind. Should he reach out and talk to them about Natalie's death? Wasn't that the noble thing to do?

He hadn't spoken to them for years now, he thought they still lived in the house in Woodbury, but maybe they'd moved. He didn't think he even had Allison's telephone number any longer, although he knew he could get it if he tried.

At the same time, he had Myles breathing down his neck about two other clients in Minnesota that were top prospects and Drake could see his point that it only made sense to work up some plans with Rick and Shay, the Minnesota support team, while he was there.

Regretting it even as he did it, Drake cancelled his round-trip, single day plane ticket. Not knowing how long he'd be gone, he thought he might as well save on the expense of a flight and a rental car and drive the six hours north and west across Wisconsin to Minneapolis.

There could be worse ways to spend a few days in August, Drake thought to himself as the door clicked shut behind him and he pressed the elevator down button in the darkened hallway.

Maybe while he was in Minnesota, he would take a few days and drive west to his parents' farm. It had been a few months since he'd visited in person.

Besides, this time of year, Minnesota was a very beautiful place.

***

A week later, as he finally turned off the interstate and headed north into one of the sprawling mini-mansion residential districts, Drake was thankful that his Minnesota team leader Rick had forewarned him not to try to cross this bridge from Bloomington over the river during rush hour traffic. At 3:00 pm, traffic was flowing nicely, and the drive went so fast he slowed his approach to Allison and Don's neighborhood and used the extra time to mentally prepare before meeting them face to face after so many years and under such difficult circumstances.

During his marriage to Natalie, Drake remembered coming to visit them only twice. He hadn't even met them before he married Natalie and the first time that he met them was in August, just after they returned from their honeymoon.

Natalie and her mother Allison, both with fiery tempers and sometimes-irrational stubborn streaks, had a falling-out and weren't on speaking terms a few months before the wedding so her parents didn't even attend the ceremony or reception.

A few weeks after they returned from their honeymoon, though, Natalie suddenly broached the topic of him meeting her mother and stepfather. Drake, having grown up in a close-knit family, was happy and relieved to finally meet his in-laws and hoped he could figure out why they were such a touchy subject with his otherwise carefree wife.

When he met them, Drake found his southern-belle mother-in-law a bit cool under her syrupy charm, but his father-in-law Don seemed affable and straightforward. The entire weekend had seemed congenial enough to Drake– they went golfing at Don and Allison's club, Allison made mimosas and Don grilled salmon - but Drake couldn't help but notice the palpable silences between Natalie and her mother that frequently underpinned the conversations.

Now, looking back, Drake recognized that he should have seen the warnings that not all was as it seemed between his beautiful wife and her sweet, genteel mother. But at the time, he was simply too much in love with his new wife and he certainly didn't want to complicate their lives together by dredging up too much family drama from her past-life.

He was complicit in allowing this fissure to simmer unattended on the hot stove that was Natalie's mind, ready to boil over along with the other past-life secrets she hid from him.

The stone walkway to Allison and Don's front door was lined with perfectly manicured shrubbery, interrupted by large ceramic pots over-flowing with greenery and bright puffs of mixed flowers. As he stepped onto the low brick porch and pressed the doorbell, Drake stepped aside to avoid the automatic sprinkler spray that watered the shrubs in front of the two-story windows on either side of the door.

His detour around the neighborhood and the extra time he spent doing it, hadn't done anything to prepare him for this conversation, he thought as he caught his reflection in the window on the right side of the front door. He looked a mess - uncertain and scared.

Drake stood up straighter and pulled back his shoulders, while trying to bolster his confidence. This was the right thing to do. He had loved Allison and Don's daughter and now that daughter was dead. Someone had to acknowledge that this had happened.

And the minor wrinkle that for years Allison and Don had suspected him of playing a part in her disappearance? Well, he couldn't let that matter. Forgiving them had been an essential step in his own redemption story.

"Hello- Drake?" Allison's surprise was evident and off-putting as she pulled open the heavy oak door and squinted at him from behind purple-framed reading glasses. Allison's long, silvery gray hair was pulled back from her pretty face and she was dressed in work-out clothes with bright pink-colored tennis shoes. One diamond-laden slender hand still held the door open while the other held a rolled-up Architectural Digest magazine.

"Yes, hello, Allison. It's been a long time, hasn't it?"

"Well, my, my. Yes, it has indeed and mightily unexpected," Her voice was soft, and her drawl was rounded as she continued to watch him, a bit suspiciously now that the initial surprise was ebbing. For a moment, she avoided his eyes and squinted slightly, as if trying to think of an excuse to get rid of him. Then, as if in resignation, she looked back at him with a guarded expression in her eyes and a fake, upturned smile on her mouth.

"Yes, well. Oh, for land's sake, my manners have escaped me, haven't they? I suppose I should ask you in?" She half-heartedly stepped back into the tiled foyer, holding the door open a bit further.

"I'm sorry to just drop in like this, Allison. I was in town on business and I just-" Drake stepped past her and then stopped in the foyer and shrugged slightly, suddenly overwhelmed with regret that he had come, "Well, it's just been a tough few months lately, you know, finding out what happened to Natalie-"

"Yaas, oh my word, that was quite a shock! Most certainly was. The police have already been here a few times to talk to us about how they found her – in that river up north. We've laid her to rest finally, bless her soul." She watched him for a long moment, as if trying to determine his motive for showing up unannounced on her doorstep after so many years. Finally, she fluttered a hand towards the kitchen located down the wide hallway at the back of the house.

"I was just fixin' to have a glass of sweet tea on the back porch. Would you like one?" As she turned and walked away, it was clear that she would prefer he not be there, but obviously, Southern hospitality was deeply embedded in her DNA, "Or, I can fix you up somethin' stronger, if you like."

As he joined her in the kitchen, she stood with eyebrows raised and one hand on the handle of the refrigerator door. As the air conditioning rippled across the over-sized granite-topped center island between them, the hairs on Drake's arms rose in an anxious shiver.

"No, iced tea is fine," Drake said, "Thank you." Feeling a bit awkward, he resisted the urge to fidget with his phone. To put the annoying habit out of his mind, he shoved the phone in his back pocket as he hulked behind her, waiting for her to pour the drinks.

"Alright then," As if Allison sensed his discomfort, her voice took on that southern motherly tone as she ordered him with another wave of her flashing fingers towards the wall of windows and wide doors that led to their patio, the space she called the back porch, "You just go ahead and make yourself comfortable out there. I'll fix up a tray and join you presently."

A few minutes of niceties were dispensed with once Allison joined him on the plush cushioned patio chairs. She updated Drake on Don's health issues (he was recovering from prostate cancer and was at a follow up doctor's appointment that afternoon) and Drake updated her on his business in Chicago and their addition of a Minneapolis office two years ago.

For a few minutes, they avoided any mention of Natalie or the recent discovery of her body. It was almost surreal how Allison could seem so unaffected by the history between them, their only link being the daughter and his ex-wife who was now considered a fugitive from the law. A dead fugitive from the law.

Drake refocused his attention on his mother-in-law who was prattling away while swishing a fly off her arm.

"– well, I don't know what could possibly be takin' Don so long today. He should've been home fifteen minutes ago," Allison regarded the Fitbit watch on her slim wrist and crossed her legs again in what Drake was beginning to see was a nervous gesture each time their conversation lagged.

It was time he took control of the conversation, he thought as he verbally shook himself. He didn't want this trip to turn out a total waste of time and energy.

"Well, actually, Allison, I'm glad to have a few minutes alone with you. I came to ask you a few questions about Natalie."

"Oh? Well, I don't know that I can answer any of your questions. As her ex-husband, you know very well that Natalie and I didn't have the typical mother-daughter relationship," Allison stopped and took a sip of her tea before continuing softly, "I loved my daughter, Drake. But one thing about that girl, she wouldn't let herself love anyone, not even her momma."

"Yes, I guess that is true-" Drake swallowed hard over an ice cube at her frank analysis of her daughter's lack of true compassion. It was a brutal reminder of how ignorant he had been during his relationship with his ex-wife.

"Well, I didn't mean for that to come out quite like that-" Allison stopped and took another long drink of her iced tea. When she set the glass down on the table next to her knee, Drake could swear her eyes looked glassier as if she had spiked her drink with something stronger. As her words slowed and her drawl deepened, he became sure that she had more than iced tea in her glass and it probably wasn't her first drink of the day.

"You know, Drake," She continued, "From the time she was a teenager, Natalie always had men sniffin' 'round about her. But, of course, that couldn't be helped, she was such a pretty thing. Most of 'em didn't mean nothin' to her though, except a couple." Allison leveled her gaze at Drake over her glass as she took another long swallow.

Fueled by whatever she'd added to her drink, Allison's thoughts could be going a million different directions, Drake realized with dread. And most of them were thoughts he was sure he was totally unprepared to hear.

"I do declare, though," She continued, her voice a little slower with each syllable, "I consider you the best catch of them all."

With her statement, Allison leaned forward in her chair and patted Drake's knee and then squeezed it with a flirty grin, and Drake's whole body contracted in shocked response at her lack of boundaries. Well, that's not at all what he expected from his mother-in-law. *Who was this person?*

"Oh, it's true," She continued with a smile that masked something steely underneath, "Don and I wished on you the worst kind of awful when we thought you had somethin' to do with her disappearin'."

Allison patted his knee again before returning to the safe space of her chair cushion three feet away from him, as Drake relaxed and unclenched his jaw, "But down deep, we knew you couldn't hurt our Natalie. Just like the others, you was swept away by her charms, that was obvious. But there was no way you could hurt her."

"No, of course not. I loved her."

"Yes, I believe you did. And she messed up mightily with you, that's the God-honest truth. Just so you know, I told her so when she told me that she had left you for that – old, rich guy. Tsk, really. He was old enough to be her father."

"I was actually wondering about that. How much did Natalie tell you about Rolph Sartell and his business?"

"Me? She didn't tell me nothin', sugar. I just had a feelin' that things was gonna end up real bad because that was her pattern. I loved my girl somethin' fierce, but the truth was, she was bad news when it came to men. When she tired of them and their money - used them up, more's the word – that was all there was to it. They was gone like a song."

Allison fluttered her fingers and nodded in slow agreement with the memories playing in her mind. Slowly, she raised her glassy eyes to Drake again, silently waiting for him to ask the obvious, follow-up question.

"The police say they can't find evidence against Rolph Sartell in her disappearance and with his fraud conviction, he'll be in prison for a long time. Who were these other men? Do you remember any names or where they live?"

"Well, I'm not sure what can be gained by askin' about them now after all this time," Allison's voice faltered, her eyes questioning him, before she continued with a hesitant tone, "There were a couple of guys when she lived in Missouri, and the guy from Indiana, right before she met you. Oh, and that guy from northern Minnesota, right after she graduated from college when she was living with her cousin Dane. Maybe one or two others-"

Wow. Each mention of a man dug the knife deeper into his gut.

So. Many. Men.

"Really? So many?" The words croaked out of his tortured mind and he dropped his eyes to regard a butterfly that was perched on the crevice between two patio stones. How could he have been so gullible, so clueless? He looked back up to see that Allison was gazing off over his shoulder, lost in her own thoughts. After a brief moment, he continued.

"Allison, do you think one of these guys would have wanted to hurt Natalie?"

"Well, of course they would," Allison snorted in the most refined way and rubbed her nose delicately afterwards as if the snort tickled her sensibilities, "Why wouldn't they? She took things from them, she didn't care 'bout nothin' or nobody. You should know, you were in the same boat as them."

"But she didn't take anything from me." Drake frowned in confusion.

"Oh, yes she did, son. She took mighty plenty from you." Quietly, she appraised him, a look of southern-style pity clouding her eyes, as she seemed to see straight into his hurt soul, "She took somethin' from everybody who ever knew her. You wouldn't be here if she hadn't taken somethin' from you."

***

His coffee was growing cold on the hotel lobby table as Drake sat with the complimentary USA Today newspaper open in front of him. Having returned from a quick trip to visit his parents and his sister's family, he had returned to the Twin Cities and finished some meetings yesterday.

It had been three days now since he visited Allison, but the short visit had been working on his mind ever since. Regretfully, he felt even more directionless than when he'd come to Minnesota in the first place.

As he played his conversation with Allison over in his mind the past few days, Drake couldn't help but feel there was more to learn. All those guys in Natalie's past, all of them likely mad at her for God only knows what. Maybe they were all victims of her scams and theft and one of them was mad enough to want her dead? Could her death have been faked to look like an accident?

Or .. another idea sidled around the corners of his consciousness, prompted by Detective Miller's line of questions. Miller seemed to think it unlikely that Natalie carried out the crime alone. So, could one of these men have been an accomplice in the crime against Rolph Sartell?

But, if so, and this really was a random car accident, why wasn't the guy found with her in the submerged vehicle? If, on the other hand, the guy wanted her dead to cut her out of the deal, why leave all that cash in the car?

Drake dropped his head into his hands and sighed deeply, trying to resolve in his mind what his next step should be. His work in Minneapolis was complete. He was free to return to Chicago.

But, still, for no rational reason, he had stayed here last night instead of driving home. It was as if he was stuck here, waiting for someone to push him one direction or another.

He had come so far, finally seeing some light again after hitting what he called his bottom that awful night almost three years ago.

That day, they had lost two clients due to the publicity surrounding his rumored involvement in her disappearance, his bank had called because someone had hacked his account (turned out his name was floating around the dark web due to the notoriety of the case) and multiple evening news teams were camped outside his condo in hot pursuit of a story after a bogus leak came out of the police investigation.

Sitting in his closet, away from the windows and the flashing lights of news vans, he had cried out to God that night. After hours of searching his soul and talking to his family on the phone, he searched his Bible for answers on what to do next.

He had always taken life as it came. He actually thrived on challenge and had always done so. But this was something completely foreign to him. The mountain was just too tall.

He admitted that night that he hadn't asked God to lead him in his life for many years, and in his futile way, he'd been trying to do it all on his own. This included his relationship with Natalie and their marriage. None of it was done with the intent to honor God and it was all exceedingly temporary.

As he read through his Bible that night, the verse Hebrews 12:27 worked on his spirit and wouldn't leave him alone for days after.

Hebrews 12:27 This means that all of creation will be shaken and removed, so that only unshakable things will remain.

Drake had experienced a complete shaking of his earthly treasure and what remained was the treasure that only God can give. It was clear to him and he relished the renewal it brought to him.

Gradually, he found a church full of people who welcomed him, and he looked back on that night as an experience that changed his life forever. Now, he didn't even feel like the same man that had married Natalie Connor so many years ago.

But living life as a Christian didn't come with a map and clear directions. When he went to God with his questions, God didn't answer plainly. Often, he didn't say anything at all.

Like in this situation with confirmation of Natalie's death, her life of lies and how he was supposed resolve all that and move forward.

One thing was clear. This indecision was beginning to cloud his mind and the nagging doubts were reminders of the days when he focused too much on himself and not enough on God.

Draining the last of his coffee, Drake gathered the loose sections of the paper together along with his empty coffee cup and turned towards the garbage can.

That was that, he thought as he resolved the next step in his mind. He'd done his duty paying his respects to Allison and now he should head home. The decision to leave Minnesota may feel a little forced, but at least it was momentum.

As he headed towards the door, his eyes landed on a stack of tourist brochures neatly lined in a plastic shelf display, the kind of brochures that were packed with activities and scenic adventures. The one that caught his attention screamed "Visit the North Shore – Lake Superior is calling you!"

He pulled one of the glossy brochures out of the display, turned it over to see the map on the back, and with his finger he traced the shoreline from Duluth, northeastward to the town of Twin Shores. It was near there that they found her. That was about all he knew.

Something about his lack of details about her death bothered him suddenly and his plan to return home of a moment ago was forgotten.

Why should he know so little about where his ex-wife died? Sure, it was a police investigation, but why should he wait for a police investigation to finish before he got more information?

Truth was, Drake was doubtful that there even would be much of an investigation since the perpetrator of the crime was found dead and the "victim" was in prison for his own long list of crimes. Plus, even if the police did figure out any of it, why would they care to tell the ex-husband?

No. Unless Drake found something out on his own that could prompt further action, he was sure he'd heard the last from Miller.

Drake traced the line on the map from the Twin Cities to Twin Shores again. He was so close - within a few hours of the place – shouldn't he at least see where it happened? Maybe that was why he hadn't felt peace about leaving Minnesota yet.

With a determined nod, Drake slipped the brochure into his suit coat pocket, hoisted his overnight bag onto his shoulder and pushed open the glass door.

He needed a little R&R and the North Shore seemed like just the place to get it.

CHAPTER 8

August 2019

Sella

"It will be just a few more minutes before I'm done with this check run, Pop, then we'll go to lunch. In the meantime, why don't you get yourself a cup of coffee and visit with the guys up front?" Sella took her father Luca by the elbow and directed him out the door of her office and towards the lobby area of the store where a small group of local men, all ranging in age from mid-forties to eight-plus, sat in chairs shooting the breeze around the coffee pot that Friday morning.

Quite the group today, Sella thought as Luca settled into a chair and she handed him a cup of coffee. Over the years, Phillip's bottomless coffee pot had become the default gathering spot once the guys had overstayed their welcome at the Kat's Coffee Shop uptown.

As she passed her older brother who stood behind the counter, Sella smiled half-heartedly at Phillip who was at the till, checking out a customer's parts order. They both knew the "look" Sella gave him – "He's yours now, please keep an eye on him."

With a last glance at her father as he attempted to join the on-going conversation between the men, Sella returned to her office to finish her work before they could leave for lunch and an afternoon off.

Proudly living and working in the area for three generations, the Lafayette family and the family-owned auto parts and repairs business were a mainstay in the small town of four thousand locals. Sella's father, Luca Lafayette, took over the original Twin Shores auto parts/repair shop after his father passed away and, with the help of his wife Violet and four children, Luca built the business to include multiple locations scattered up the north shore and across the arrowhead to the iron range.

Luca, reminiscent of his French-Canadian father, had a big personality and even bigger plans for his family. As his sons grew into adults, he incorporated each of them into managing a store and, alongside her mother Violet, Sella managed the books. Everything was going pretty much according to Luca's plans until a few years ago when it suddenly began to unravel.

First, her mother succumbed to liver cancer after a tortuous battle and then, within months of his wife's death, Luca began forgetting things.

At first the forgetfulness was sporadic, and the lapses were inconsequential things like appointments at the dentist and paying the electric bill. Then, it became common that Luca would forget names of customers and their families and at the same time, his grasp of the business operations and finances began to falter.

Attributing Luca's sudden memory losses and general cognitive haze to symptoms of depression at the loss of his wife, his children began to compensate in the business by combining efforts into a more centralized system and, in addition to her role as Finance

Manager at the business, Sella took on an active, care-giving role for her seventy-four year old father.

The eventual Alzheimer's diagnosis two years ago felt like a weight dropped on the family, even though by then it was no surprise to any of Luca's adult children.

But, still. Hearing the physician's diagnosis that day and watching her strong, proud father react to it with tears in his eyes, left Sella desperately adrift in her mind - like she was disengaged from her tether, adrift far from shore on the squally waters of Lake Superior, no land in sight.

That awful day in the doctor's office, Sella grasped her father's once-sturdy fingers tightly, trying to offer him consolation. As she searched the deep lines of his troubled face, the realization hit full force that her father had always been the rock of the family. They had all lived in his orbit.

But now that rock had become loosened and it became clear that he was something *less* than he had been her whole life – he seemed *smaller and finite* in a weird way.

When she met his trembling gaze, Sella glimpsed a depth of humanity in her father that she'd never witnessed before. He wasn't the all-knowing, always in control, larger-than-life father anymore. He was just a man, like any other. And he needed her now as never before.

As the days and months wore on, the hard truth became plain - her father Luca was disappearing. Sella began to ruminate over the eventual reality of Alzheimer's disease - at one point he would be completely gone, his mind somewhere far away, and he could do nothing about it. They could do nothing about it except pray for strength to deal with the day to day loss.

To contemplate this desperate future felt like Death to Sella. So, instead of succumbing to this fatalistic, living death-sentence, she did whatever she could to make the most of his time with them.

She convinced her father to sell his house in Twin Shores and move out to her house in the woods, near the river. Now, hers and her son Henri's lives had become inextricably intertwined with her father's life.

It wasn't easy. It wasn't exciting or glamorous. There wasn't much room for pondering the future or reveling in the past. She cherished the moments for what they were.

Fleeting. The moments of this life were fleeting, like the sea gulls gliding over the lake. There one moment, gone the next.

Before Sella realized it, a half hour had gone by and she hurriedly clicked shut her laptop, shoved it in her work bag and grabbed her purse, feeling guilty for leaving her father out front with Phillip, who was always busy with customers and phone calls.

Stopping in the hallway at the employee time clock to review who was scheduled to work Saturday, Sella dropped her bags on the floor and listened in on the conversation happening in the lobby area around the corner from where she stood.

"-I don't know who he is, Phillip, he was just asking for Luca, so I told him that was Luca over there sitting on the bench with his grandson." Dell Wilson said as he joined Phillip at the counter, the fuse he was planning to return still in his hand.

Curious about the verbal exchange, Sella joined the men in the lobby and glanced out towards the parking lot where a stranger with closely clipped blonde hair and neatly trimmed dark beard stood talking to Luca and Henri. The man who was wearing sunglasses, was tanned and nice looking, probably in his mid-to-late thirties and seemed mild enough with his light gray golf shorts and bright white shirt. Probably a tourist, Sella guessed; the town overflowed with them at this time of year.

"I'll go see what he needs, Phillip." Sella announced as she passed the counter and pushed open the door. Something about this encounter seemed slightly amiss. Over the course of the past few years, after Sella had taken on the care-giver role for her father, she was quite sure she knew most things about him and his life.

Having a stranger ask for Luca by name? That was a little strange.

"Hello, can I help you?" Sella called protectively from a few feet away, interrupting Luca mid-sentence. The stranger turned in surprise and then glanced back at Luca, a slightly confused look settling on his engaging face and in his boyish half-smile.

"Well, I was just asking Luca and Henri some questions and they were kindly helping me out-" The man spoke, his attention focused on her again, his smile lifting further in a friendly grin.

"Sella, he wants to see where we found the car. You remember the car in the river, Sella. Right? You remember-" Luca nodded emphatically as if by repeating the memory out loud would make it stick in his mind and Sella's mind simmered as her defenses kicked in. Was this guy another annoying press person or was he some quack blogger just looking for another angle on the dead woman story?

"Yes, Pop. I remember." She said as patiently as she could and then reached for Henri's shoulders, drawing him closer to her protectively. Slowly, now that she was closer to him, she regarded the stranger with suspicion.

"May I ask, are you with the press or law enforcement or something?" Sella appraised his clothing with a critical eye. He sure wasn't dressed very professionally - his tan, fit legs looked like a runner, or someone who played a lot of golf. Maybe this casual attire was part of his disguise to get information.

"No, I'm not," He offered his hand graciously, "I'm staying at Carolynn's bed and breakfast in town and she told me to come here to talk to Luca. My name's Drake Connor. I'm from Chicago."

Still bristling inside at his presumption and Carolynn Greenfeld for telling him to come here, Sella wanted to ignore his handshake but found herself unable to withstand the charm of his guileless smile. Reaching out from behind Henri, she shook his hand and then drew Henri closer to her side again. He still hadn't told her why he was here asking questions.

"Well, Mr. Connor," Sella said, keeping her voice cool, "I'm sorry, but whoever you are, we can't help you. We don't know anything about the car or the woman they found in it."

"But, Sella," Luca spoke up suddenly, as if trying to be helpful, "We do know where they found her! We could show him where we found her, couldn't we?" Luca ended his statement and shuffled his feet on the pavement as a familiar glaze passed over his face.

73

Sella knew the expression and the pattern well. Already, in Luca's mind, he was doubting that he could remember where they found the car. In fact, he probably didn't remember what the man had asked him to start this conversation only a few minutes ago.

"Yeah, we could show him-" Henri offered, then clamped his mouth shut when he saw his mother's icy expression.

"I would be so grateful if you would take the time to do that," Drake Connor offered with a hesitant half smile, "I have come up here hoping to see where she- was found." He finished his statement awkwardly, obviously adjusting the sentence to avoid the word "died."

Something about his hesitation made Sella pause and she felt a trickle of thaw encroach her reserve towards the guy. Who was he really and why was he here?

"Why? Are you family to her?" Sella asked.

"Well, yes, I guess I am. I was married to Natalie."

From behind the rimmed sunglasses, Drake Connor held Sella's gaze as the full realization of his words hit her hard. Suddenly, the faceless, person-less woman had a name and a family.

Henri's eyes darted from the man to his mother and back again as he gulped in surprise and Luca suddenly stopped shuffling his feet and stared at the man. A moment of stunned silence passed between them before Sella found her voice.

"Oh, I'm sorry to hear that, Mr. Connor. I'm really sorry to hear that."

"Thank you. But, honestly, we were divorced at the time of the accident. She had already remarried. But still-" Drake hesitated as he looked down at the pavement before he spoke again. As if he had decided that being honest was the best way to get what he wanted, he continued softly, "I guess I would just like to see where it happened. Just so I know where she was. You know?"

Yes, Sella thought, she understood completely.

When her husband Garrett left her three years ago, the separation and eventual divorce was sudden and unexpected. It knifed her straight through and she became a caricature of her former self, like a walking wounded version, just barely getting by each day.

But when, a year later, Garrett was killed in a plane crash the emotional blow to her and Henri was not only because of his physical death, it was the death of a dream. The dream that someday, against all odds and past hurt, they could work it out and become a family again.

The similarities in hers and Drake Connor's life experiences were striking. Both divorced and both of their spouses now dead.

But, because of their custody arrangement, at least she was informed right away after Garrett was killed. From the articles she had read on the internet and what Coop had shared with her about the investigation, this woman – Natalie – had been considered a missing person for four years before her car turned up in the river. So that meant that Drake Connor had never known where she was. And divorce aside, if he was still in love with his ex-wife, did he live every day wondering where she was, and would she ever return?

"Okay, Mr. Connor," Sella spoke finally, a slow warm feeling inching its way over her heart, "Follow us. We'll show you where Natalie was."

CHAPTER 9

1998-2000

Natalie

I followed him.

My mom knew it was only a matter of time before I would follow him to Arizona. She told people that I "ran away" because that sounded less trashy to her country club friends, but she knew the whole time where I was, and she never once asked me to return. In a letter to me, she told me she was "shaking the rug" and from now on, I was on my own.

I didn't think about any of the long-term consequences to leaving home and moving in with my boyfriend. It didn't make any difference to me that I wasn't eighteen yet or finished with high school. I didn't think about the future.

That first year, we lived in an off-campus apartment near TC's university. We told people, including the local high school in Phoenix where I finished my senior year, that our parents were dead and that I was his adopted sister. Each small wrinkle that cropped up with the school or neighbors and friends, we bluffed our way through.

TC was making good money on his various credit card scams and he was figuring out ways to create identities with social security numbers and passports. Being so close to the US/Mexico border helped and soon his business was taking so much of his time, he was barely spending any time studying.

It was through the fake identity business that TC met Tyrone Pire.

Tyrone owned a construction business that did dirt and concrete work for new residential districts in the Phoenix/Mesa area. TC helped Tyrone's workers become "legitimate" citizens and Tyrone helped TC pay for college expenses.

Soon, while he was still a student, TC was working full time for Tyrone's company. He became his "assistant." He wasn't like the typical assistant though - not like the person who handles the above-board office details of running a business. Instead, TC was the guy who handled all those details that "no one else needed to know."

I used to watch with fascination how TC wound his way deeper and deeper into Tyrone's affairs. He was only in his early twenties after all, still a college student, but that didn't seem to matter at all to Tyrone.

Whatever Tyrone wanted – a separate set of falsely inflated invoices for a job, a way to hide funds from his business investors, a set of false financials to get low interest government loans – TC did it all for him and never once questioned Tyrone about the ethics of it.

I sometimes would ask TC what he expected to get out of this arrangement – he had other ways to pay his college expenses and he certainly wasn't cut out to be a loyal employee at Tyrone's company long term.

TC just told me that he was "baiting the hook" and that someday he would "set it so deep that the fish had no choice but to submit to his fate."

Life sailed along like this for a while until that day in June 2000 when TC told me that he had a plan to finish his degree at UNC Charlotte and that he was leaving town in three days.

When I freaked out at the sudden change, he told me it was safest for me not to ask too many questions. All he would tell me was that the hook had been set and he had to leave, and I could come with him if I wanted to. Or, stay in Arizona by myself, it was my choice. He said he wouldn't force me to do anything that I didn't want to.

Of course, I followed him. It didn't matter to me that I was enrolled for the upcoming fall semester at a local college in Phoenix.

After we had safely landed in Charlotte, North Carolina, TC told me that he had embezzled more than $100,000 from Tyrone Pire's company over the past eight months. And the beauty of it? All the money came from the ill-gotten gains of Tyrone's various schemes, so nothing was "recorded" and the likelihood of him reporting the theft was non-existent.

I was surprised by the shake-down because he'd never mentioned it to me, of course. But I have to say I wasn't shocked that he would do it.

What did surprise me was the size of it. And I was awed by the nerve it took and the confidence he had in his ability to get away with it.

As we walked through the airport, my mind was spinning with the knowledge that my boyfriend had just ripped someone off in a huge way and we were now fugitives. In a daze, I watched as people ate their tacos at airport restaurants and stood in line at the restrooms just going about their boring lives while my life seemed so surreal, like a movie. Or a dream. I remember thinking, it's just too crazy, maybe none of this was really happening.

It was when we approached the rental car counter and TC gave a different name for the reservation that the realization of my life's new trajectory really hit home. That's when I saw his new driver's license and heard that he was no longer TC.

Tony Carmine had been replaced by Anthony Tyrone.

How ironic was that? Hijacking the name of his victim. Sweet!

That was the moment.

I fell in love with him that moment. I didn't care what name he called himself.

CHAPTER 10

2019

Drake

The trees. So many trees.

Each mile they drove deeper into it, the forest seemed to tighten its grip, suffocating in its nearness and silence. The trees were so close to the road that their hulking presence encroached into the roadway which had been resolutely cut through the forest at one time but was gradually being swallowed up again by forces of nature.

Growing up on a farm in the rolling fields of southwestern Minnesota and now living in the heart of Chicago, Drake was unfamiliar with the desolate stillness of a place such as this, with its natural landmarks with names like Devil's Kettle Falls, Pincushion Mountain and Caribou Trail hidden within the cloak of its towering pines.

It freaked him out, if he was honest. It was just a little too quiet – way too much solitude - in this place commonly referred to as Minnesota's Arrowhead region. This kind of seclusion prompted a person to think about things. And he'd probably been thinking too much lately.

It was time to move on from Natalie.

Of course, he knew that. He had felt the shift coming on for about a year now. Every time he prayed about it, he felt lighter somehow. And he knew that he could trust God with it all.

Then, they found her in that river and the insecure, hazy gray feelings started to rise again. They were like a whisper in his soul, insisting that something about Natalie still haunted him.

For some reason, he felt if he could only see where she'd been the last few years, he would be one step closer to putting this behind him. Lucky for him, upon arriving in Twin Shores, the task of finding out where Natalie's car was found hadn't taken long because everyone so far had been surprisingly helpful.

In the thorough overview he'd gotten from the Carolynn Greenfeld, the friendly and very talkative owner of the bed and breakfast he was staying at, he found out about the two people who came upon the car in the river. According to Carolynn Greenfeld, Luca Lafayette was the patriarch of a family-owned car parts and repair business, now run by his three adult sons and one daughter and that Natalie's car was found near his home in the woods outside of town.

The chatty innkeeper had omitted to mention that Luca had a memory condition, however, and Drake surmised it was either dementia or Alzheimer's disease. Almost immediately upon meeting Luca, Drake recognized some of the signs of Alzheimer's that his grandfather had displayed prior to his death six years earlier.

As Drake noticed in his grandfather, even as the disease robbed a person's memories, it often exaggerated other aspects of the person's personality. Meeting Luca earlier – his Twins baseball hat pulled low over a thick mane of gray hair and a ready smile in his dark brown eyes - it was obvious he was a gregarious guy with a sharp sense of humor. He must have been quite a force in his day, given the family business he built.

His grandson Henri seemed to be picking up similar traits. In the brief conversation he had with two of them before Sella joined them, Drake was drawn immediately to the boy who seemed reserved and quiet, but also had a slightly mischievous look on his freckled face when he talked about the woods near their house and the river that ran through them.

Henri was just getting into the story about how he found Natalie's car when mama bear Sella came out and joined them. Although there was no way for Drake to know, it became clear from Sella's demeanor that Luca and Henri must have become subjects of unwanted attention with their discovery of Natalie's car last spring. As soon as she started questioning him, Drake could tell Mama Bear had her claws out and was ready to fight. After the third degree she gave him, he had to admit, he was rather surprised when she softened up enough to lead him out here.

And the bear analogy seemed to fit, just look where they lived. There had to be tons of bear around here. As he rolled down his window to enjoy the woodsy aroma of the pines from within the safe confines of his car, Drake smiled to himself.

She was quite the protective mother, that Sella Sommers. Carolynn Greenfeld had mentioned something about Sella living with her father out in the woods. No mention of a husband, so she must be a single mother, Drake surmised.

Glancing around at the pristine, remote beauty of the landscape surrounding him, Drake wondered at the strength it took to be a single mother living out here during the depths of northern Minnesota winters and the perils of forest fires during dry spells in summer.

Not to mention the hazards of sharing your backyard with black bear and timber wolves.

On the road ahead of him, near a bridge, Sella's Jeep pulled slowly over to the side of the road and she stepped out of the driver's side door and waited on the road's shoulder as Drake pulled in behind them.

That's when Drake noticed the sudden burning sensation rolling around in his gut.

This must be the place. This was the river where Natalie died.

As he got out of his car, Drake glanced at his surroundings and filtered through the questions in his mind.

Did they get so much snow around here that Natalie could just drive off this road and no one would see tracks or see the car in the river below?

How could they not see her car in this river for *four* years?

Where did this road lead anyway?

And why was she on it?

Why was she even in Minnesota in the first place–

"Mr. Connor," Sella's voice interrupted his frantic mind traffic and Drake glanced towards her, grateful that someone else was here with him on this lonely stretch of road, "I told Henri that he could take you down the embankment over there to the place where he found her car."

As he acknowledged the direction she pointed, Drake glanced towards the passenger seat and noticed Luca was sound asleep with his face turned towards the sunlight streaming through the side window. Even the steady hum of birds in the trees all around them didn't seem to stir him awake.

"Yeah, Dad is asleep. This must have been too much excitement for one day." Sella smiled lovingly towards her father and then turned as Henri joined her at the front of the car, "But that's okay. Henri probably knows this river better than Dad does. Isn't that right, Henri?"

"Yeah, I guess so. It's pretty cool around here. Come on, it was this way."

The boy started across the road as Drake glanced again at Sella, the quiet between them interrupted by the caw of a nearby black bird.

"Thanks for doing this, Sella. I really do appreciate it." Drake smiled at her, grateful that she was willing to help him.

"Of course, no problem. Henri knows his way around - he'll show you where it was and then we'll be on our way. Do you think you can get back to town okay?" She swept some bangs away from her face and her brow furrowed, a natural concern filling her sable-brown eyes.

Drake held her gaze for a moment before he found his voice to answer her. Something about Sella made a person look twice, something about her was – he searched for the word in his mind – intriguing. *She was intriguing.*

"Ah -yes, yes of course," Drake stumbled over his response as he tried to refocus his mind on the task at hand.

"Okay, then. It's that way-" Sella pointed again across the road towards the embankment where Henri patiently knelt in the ditch, engrossed, as he watched the river rush under the bridge.

"Yeah, okay. Thanks, Sella."

She nodded, smiled, and opened her door to the Jeep while Drake focused his eyes on the river that took the life of his ex-wife.

Sella

Saturdays were the best days of the week, according to Henri. Especially if they included blueberry pancakes for breakfast and ice cream at Art's Dairy & Dine, the drive-in ice cream shop in Twin Shores. This particular Saturday, he got both.

"I think my absolute favorite flavor this year is Cookie Crumbles. Is that your favorite too, Poppy?" Henri questioned his grandfather as he swiped a big lop off his ice cream cone. Each summer, Art's introduced limited edition unique flavors of homemade ice cream with names like Salt & Peppermint and Fudge Factory.

"Well, yes, I think so," Luca wiped his mouth with a napkin, a confused look passing over his face, "Have I ever tried that one, Sella?"

"Yes, you did. The last time we were here you had that one. But I think your favorite is Chocolate Covered Cherry. That one's pretty good too, isn't it?"

Sella smiled as her father finished his cone and added his crumpled napkin to the red plastic tray sitting in front of him on the picnic table.

Even under Art's awning, the early evening was still warmed by the simmering sun and Sella shifted her sunglasses more securely on her nose. The drive-in was busy this evening and their dinner had been stretched longer because of the many friends that had stopped by to visit their table during the evening.

As she gathered their tray of empty cups and napkins and walked towards the garbage can, Sella noticed a familiar figure sitting at a table a few feet away, his back towards them.

Drake Connor. Dressed casually again this time in navy blue golf shorts and a lightweight jacket, he was eating dinner alone.

Eating alone, she pondered. In a strange town on a Saturday evening, finding himself all alone on the quest to find closure over the death of his ex-wife.

Sella looked sideways at her father and Henri. They seemed oblivious to Drake sitting there but she supposed the neighborly thing to do would be to go over and say hello.

Sella wasn't sure why she hesitated in her mind about doing so. It was completely against her nature to hold back like this with people. Certainly, the guy deserved a friendly greeting. After taking him out to the river yesterday, he wasn't a perfect stranger any longer.

As they walked by his table on their way to their car, Sella stopped.

"Hello, Drake. How are things with you today?"

"Well, hello! Good. Things are good." He nodded as he set down his iced tea and smiled up at them in surprise. "You guys enjoying a night out on the town, huh?"

"Yeah, we like Art's," Henri spoke up, immediately comfortable with his new friend, "They have the best ice cream in the whole state!"

"Really?" Drake looked down at his tray with a half-eaten burger and fries, "Well then, I guess I'll have to order some ice cream for dessert. Thanks for the tip, Henri."

"Sure thing," Henri said and then his eyes lit with excitement, oblivious to the somber reason that Drake asked them to show him the river, "Hey, Drake, did the beaver show up while you were at the river yesterday?"

"Ah, no, Henri, they didn't," Drake smiled graciously, seemingly not upset, "I was there for a while, but I didn't see any beaver moving around, sorry. I saw a raccoon though. He climbed a tree right in front me and just watched me for the longest time from about 30 feet up. That was pretty cool." Drake laughed and then continued, "But I suppose you see that stuff all the time. No big deal for you, huh?"

"Yeah, I have seen raccoons before. Even baby raccoons. I should show you the place where I find minnows. And there's this hollowed out log on the bank, I've seen mink going in and out of it so it must be where they live-"

"Well, that all sounds like fun, Henri," Sella interrupted before Henri embarrassed him with more invitations that Drake certainly

87

wasn't interested in accepting, "But I'm sure Drake will be going home soon, won't you?"

"Actually, I've booked a vacation rental in Twin Shores and I plan to stay for a few weeks," Drake smiled easily at the group of them, "I haven't had a vacation in- well, it's been years. I want to go hiking, do some sight-seeing, so I decided to stay a while."

"Oh, that's great!" Luca spoke up, "We have all kinds of hiking trails around here. Sella loves to hike, and Henri does too. They'd be happy to show you around. And I can show you some good fishing spots, if you're interested."

"Well, Dad, I'm sure Drake already has his vacation planned." Sella tried to offer another escape route for Drake, certain now that he would feel overwhelmed with their enthusiasm for his company.

"I just might take you up on that, if you have the time-" Drake raised his eyebrows to Sella and smiled at Henri and Luca.

"Say, why don't you come out to the house tonight?" Luca continued speaking, his face animated. Sella hadn't seen him this happy for a long time. It was obvious his inner extrovert was coming out. "I can show you what I have for fishing equipment. You're welcome to use mine, if you want."

"Oh, well- sure – if that's okay with you, Sella."

Each time she'd given him an out, Drake refused to take it, she noticed. Maybe he really did want some company on his vacation. Even if they were strangers. *What an unusual guy.*

"Sure. Why not?" Sella smiled thinly but couldn't help wondering if this was a good idea, "Come on out. You drove right past our place last night when you went to the river. We're the driveway with the wooden bear mailbox about a mile before the bridge. We'll see you later."

***

"–so is it kind of spooky living out here, just the three of you?" Drake uncorked the bottle of chardonnay and poured her a glass.

The evening had gone by so quickly that Sella was shocked to notice the late hour on the clock. No wonder that Luca had started to drift off to sleep in his leather chair and Henri was rubbing his eyes and yawning.

After they finalized a plan to go fishing with Drake after church the next day, her father and son ambled off to bed, leaving Sella and Drake in the kitchen alone with Sella wondering how to politely usher him out the front door.

Even though, secretly, she didn't really want him to leave.

Drake was an easy conversationalist, interesting and funny. An avowed single mother, Sella was too busy to consider a romantic relationship with a man and she hadn't encouraged any either. But she was surprised by the friendly comradery she felt with Drake.

And, she had to admit, it was comforting to have a man, besides her dad or her brothers, in the house again. Even if he was just a tourist passing through, he was good company. So, when he held up the bottle of wine that he'd brought along with him and questioned if she was interested in sharing a glass with him, she'd not hesitated for a moment.

"Not really," She answered his question frankly and motioned him to follow her out to the screened back porch, "We don't think of it as spooky. We're used to living alongside all the wild creatures. You might even find over the next couple of weeks that this place grows on you."

Breathing in the scents of the pine needles and the damp, woodsy earth coming through the screen, she snuggled deep into the plump cushioned chair set in the corner of the porch and kicked her feet up onto the ottoman. Sella watched him take a long, relaxed breath as he sank into the chair alongside her's.

"Well, it is wild country, that's for sure," He listened, his eyes squinting as he concentrated, "I don't think I could hear a car on the road if I tried. The birds and crickets are too loud."

"Ha, yeah. That's right. I'm so used to it, I forget that other places don't sound like this."

"Well, not *my* place anyway," He smiled and took a swallow of his wine.

"Yes, I've been there. Chicago is a world away – and *also* a very nice place to call home." She finished generously, trying to hide her feelings that a city was likely the last place she could ever see herself calling home.

"Yeah, Chicago's a great place. It's where I live and work, but I don't know if I consider it my home."

"Really? Haven't you lived there a long time?"

"Yes, for many years now. But, it's- oh, I don't know-" Drake looked out over the yard and then back again, "For some reason, lately I'm not feeling – at home – there."

"Hmm, I guess that happens sometimes." Sella murmured noncommittally. She couldn't really imagine that feeling. All she'd ever known was this place as her home.

"Yeah, maybe. With our business, I feel tied there but honestly, I really wanted to get out years ago. You know, after-" Drake hesitated briefly and took another swallow of his wine. He looked at Sella as he set his glass down next to the day-old newspaper on the table next to him.

"You know, Sella," His voice had a nice timbre to it, low and sure, and he regarded her seriously as he spoke, "I've noticed that you haven't asked me anything about Natalie. People usually do that right away."

"Do they? I guess I feel like that's *your* business and none of *my* business."

"That's noble, thank you." Drake paused and looked as if he was debating something in his mind before he continued, "It's strange, but I think it's because you haven't asked me that I really want to tell you about her."

"Then go ahead. What do you want to tell me about Natalie?"

"Well, if you search our names on Google, you won't read anything about the real us. We were happily married for a while – well, I thought we were happily married anyway – until she started an affair with her boss. That led to our divorce."

Drake paused, picked up his glass again and took another drink before continuing, his silvery eyes glinted like stars in the darkening, setting sunlight filtering through the screened windows.

"So, Rolph and Natalie got married and after a while, I'm basically out of her life altogether. Suddenly, I have detectives show up at my door asking me questions about where she is and what do I know about her stealing money from her husband's company."

"Really? Wow..." Sella couldn't imagine that happening in real life, with real people. It was like something from a movie.

"Yeah. That's when it gets really crazy. Natalie just disappeared off the face of planet after she embezzled a ton of money from him. At first, they suspected him of being involved in her disappearance. Then they turned to me. Hardcore. It was big news in Chicago at the time – the ex-husband is the prime suspect in his ex-wife's disappearance. They even theorized that we planned the theft together. But, since I hadn't talked to her for almost a year, that theory didn't go very far."

"I can't imagine," Sella paused, shocked even further as she imagined the man sitting next to her the subject of a police investigation. Still, the logical question was one she couldn't help asking, "But, weren't you were married to her for a while? Did you ever suspect she could do something like that?"

"You mean steal money from her husband and then vanish without a trace?" Drake smoothed his beard, a look of bewilderment on his handsome face as he shook his head, "No. I had no clue."

"Wow." There were no words to respond to that. *How does one not know that you spouse is capable of something like that?*

"Yeah, I think that's why I had to come here - to see for myself the place where she was found and talk to the people who found her – for it to be *real*. Nothing about any of it has ever felt real."

"Well, I hope coming here helps you sort it out." Sella took a drink from her wineglass hoping she was saying something that would offer some degree of comfort.

"You know, surprisingly, it has helped. Even though my name has been cleared now, I still have questions about why this all happened. I can't seem to let go of questions about why she was here in the first place. It's all so random. Where was she going? Was someone else involved in this? I don't know, I just have so many questions."

He looked at her with that burning intense gaze and she found herself wanting to help him in some way.

"Have you tried talking to her family? Or maybe some of her friends?"

"I've done some of that," He replied, "but I guess you had to know her to understand; she wasn't like most normal people. Natalie was an island onto herself. Her father died when she was young, and she wasn't close to her mother or stepfather. Basically, I was her family."

"Well, I'm sure with time you will come up with some answers." Sella recognized her words were a feeble attempt, but what else could a person to say to someone who was in his situation? An experience like his was bound to alter everything in your life, who you trust and how you love.

"Yeah, that's what I'm hoping to do over the next few weeks -just get some distance from work and see where this goes. At least now I can say the heavy load of it all seems to be lifting."

"I'm impressed by you, Drake," Sella said impulsively, a surge in her spirit prompting her to continue, "With all you've gone through, you don't seem bitter."

"Ohh, I have my moments, trust me. But I really try to focus on what's important – my faith in God, my family and friends, my work. The way I've come to see it, each day is a portion of our life on our way to heaven. I need to spend each portion wisely."

"Very true." Something about his pronouncement of his faith was in equal parts bold and vulnerable and Sella felt an immediate kinship with his statement. It would make the conversation much more intimate, but she would enjoy a deeper discussion of how his faith carried him through these struggles. Instead, however, he abruptly changed the subject.

"So. That's my story and my quest, Sella. Will you tell me some of your story?" The stars that were his eyes seemed to be twinkling as he raised his glass to her.

"Oh, okay," She sat up straighter in her chair, slightly uncomfortable that he was so intentionally focused on her, "Well, there isn't much to tell – besides what you already know. I'm a mom and daughter and I work for the family business. I live in the woods with bear, wolves and raccoons that climb trees– not much to tell besides that." She found herself smiling when he laughed at her joke.

"I'm sure there's more than that. What about Henri's dad? Is he in the picture?" Drake looked down, ostensibly to shoo away a fly but Sella knew it was for her benefit.

Okay, here we go, she thought. *We're going to have that conversation.*

"No," she replied, "not since he died almost two years ago."

"Oh, I'm sorry-" His brow furrowed in concern.

"Don't worry about it," She interrupted graciously, "how were you to know? I guess Carolynn Greenfeld didn't get around to telling you about Henri's father?"

"Ah, no," Drake smiled ruefully, "I guess she didn't."

"Well, most people around here don't talk about it. I guess it's out of respect...or pity. They avoid it not because Garrett died though. It's because a year before he died, he left us and moved halfway across the country. Because of Henri's child support, our attorney was notified when Garrett's estate went through probate. That's how we found out Henri's dad had died."

"Oh boy. That's tough, Sella." Drake sat forward in his chair, and folded his hands in front of him, as if to stop himself from reaching out to her.

"Yeah, it was." Sella paused as a pang twisted in the middle of her chest, "It still is sometimes." She finished simply, tipped her glass for the last swallow of wine and stood up from her chair, hoping he would take the hint as a signal of dismissal.

"I bet." Drake looked up at her from his seat, holding her gaze for a long moment before smiling tenderly and standing. He held his unfinished wine glass towards her, making it obvious that he didn't really want to leave but he was taking the hint, "Well, time to go. Thanks for everything, Sella. You have a great family and I appreciate all you're doing to help me with this."

"No problem," Sella said over her shoulder as she walked through the darkened kitchen and set their wine glasses on the counter. Flipping on lights as she continued through the house to the front door, she hoped he was following behind her - but not too close, she was starting to feel jumpy around him, "We'll see you tomorrow at noon sharp. The forecast sounds perfect for fishing."

She turned as she reached the front door and found him standing behind her, not too close, just friendly-close.

"I look forward to it. Good night." He said as he lifted his hand in a half wave and walked past her.

The shimmer of the dim porch lamp slivered through the inky dark summer sky and reflected off the chrome of his vehicle that sat quietly in her driveway. As he reached for the driver's side door, he smiled at her, the bright shimmer of which shown like a light through the shadows.

It was that image, that bright smile, that stuck with her long after she hit the pillow that night. As she tossed in bed, repeatedly puffing her pillow to fit "just right" under her neck, Sella's mind wandered over what Drake Connor had shared with her.

Who was this guy really? Could he be trusted? His story seemed so unbelievable and completely foreign when compared to her routine, rather bland, life. She had a vulnerable father and an impressionable young son to protect, perhaps she was being naïve and too trusting of this tourist.

But something about him seemed genuine. When he spoke, he was direct, he looked you in the eye and he didn't seem to be concocting his next sentence in his head before he spoke. He seemed truthful and authentic.

And she had to admit, it was interesting, this quest of his and the mystery surrounding his ex-wife. If he was willing to share some of his very personal journey with complete strangers, what harm could come of them (*well, really, her*) helping him out a bit?

Maybe she could ask more questions of Coop. Not that he'd be willing to compromise the investigation of course, but he might tell her something that would be meaningful to Drake.

Feeling settled in her mind, Sella turned on her right side to face the silvery moonlight shining through her window, plumped the pillow one last time and finally found sleep.

CHAPTER 11

2019

Drake and Sella

"When I was a kid, I liked to fish too. We spent a lot of time working on the farm, but we got away as much as we could to our family's lake cabin near Park Rapids."

"I could tell you know your way around a boat." Sella reached for the door handle on the garage refrigerator and set the container of cleaned fish on the rack inside. Since her dad and Henri had joined her brother Phillip's family for an overnight stay at their lake house after their afternoon of fishing, their catch of walleye would have to be cooked up another day.

"Well, I can tell you that at his age, I was nowhere near as accomplished as Henri is at netting a fish. That kid's amazing!"

Drake spoke from across the garage where he expertly flipped the boat's dust cover across the stern.

"Ha, yeah, but then like he says, all he needs to do is go low and lift high. Dad's taught him well, hasn't he?" Sella joined him from her side of the boat, and they pulled the cover over the seats together.

"I'll say!" Drake paused as he pulled the straps tight around the boat motor and then stood straight as he set his hands on his hips, "So, now that everything's put away and the "boys" are otherwise occupied, can I convince you to join me for a beer and a sandwich at one of the places in town? Or, do you have plans for this evening?"

"Ah, no, I guess not," Sella did a quick calculation in her head about the safety of her next comment and then decided to trust her gut, Drake had been nothing but friendly all afternoon, "But, how about we just eat here? I could put some of that walleye on the grill."

"Even better! But let me help with the grilling. I'm rotten in the kitchen but I'm fairly decent with a grill." Smiling as he bent to open the cooler, Drake loaded his arms with cans of left-over sodas and snacks. Glad that she'd suggested it, Sella opened the refrigerator again and retrieved the fillets. She would enjoy the company for dinner.

***

Sella set the cup of steaming coffee in front of him on the kitchen island as he smiled his thanks. He was reminded again how comfortable he found it here in Minnesota, with Sella and her family. Finding good people in such a random, unexpected way bolstered his faith that God was taking notice of his circumstances. Even if his life had been marked by some suffering, there were still simple pleasures to be had - like an incredibly delicious dinner of grilled walleye fillets and great conversation with a new friend.

Choosing a chair across from him, Sella sat down and sipped from her mug, strangely quiet after their lively banter during dinner. Not quite sure how to read her yet - as he tried not to stare at her captivating face - he waited, wondering what was on her mind.

"So, Drake," Sella spoke tentatively, as if she was unsure how to approach the topic, "I understand if you'd rather not tell me, but have you thought of any next steps in learning more about Natalie?"

Surprised by her interest and a bit uncomfortable, Drake set his cup on the counter and filtered through his reaction. Was it possible that for a moment, after enjoying his time with her so much, that he had forgotten what had brought him to Minnesota in the first place?

Of course, Sella hadn't forgotten.

He tried to look at it from her perspective. To her, he was an outsider, someone with a sketchy past and maybe not trustworthy. Even if she thought that, she was making an effort to be nice and it made him feel good that she cared enough to ask.

"Yes, actually," He replied honestly even though he found it hard to look her directly in the eyes, "Tuesday I will be going to Duluth to meet with a cousin of hers that lives there. Years ago, Natalie went to the U of M-Duluth and she lived with Dane while she went to school. It's a long shot, but it's the only connection I can think of that might explain why she was here."

"That might make sense, we're not that far from Duluth. Do you think he might have been involved in the theft?"

"I don't know. When I knew him there were a few skirmishes with the law, but I don't think he was too shady. 'Course I have a dismal track record on judging people's character."

Sella smiled weakly at his comment, as if she agreed with him completely. He could tell she was confused by his cluelessness and utter lack of judgement when it came to Natalie.

"There were a few other people that Natalie's mom Allison mentioned to me, but I don't have names. I guess I will talk to Dane first and see where that goes."

"What will you do if you suspect he's involved?" Sella asked, smoothing a curl of hair behind her ear.

"I suppose I will go to the authorities."

"Okay. Well, I know the local sheriff if you decide you want to go that route." She said, as if she was eager to help.

"Of course, you do." Drake teased, enjoying the flush that lit her eyes and pinkened the tops of her cheeks.

"Well, not that I make a habit of breaking the law or anything," She laughed, and Drake warmed at the sound of it. Almost shyly, she broke the look between them and continued, "Coop – Sheriff Cooper – and I grew up together. He's been a friend of my brother's since they were kids and his wife Val and family attend the same church as we do. Typical small town, everyone knows everyone."

"That type of friend can come in handy – if you ever make it a habit to start breaking the law, I mean." Drake teased her again, wanting desperately to keep the smile from leaving her mouth.

"Yeah, right. I don't think he'd let anyone off the hook, friend or not. He's always been a "by the book" kind of guy."

"Well, good to know. So, I guess if I get stopped for speeding, it wouldn't help to drop your name."

"No, sorry, wouldn't help you a bit. It might even work against you; he feels very protective about us living out here. And you're a stranger in these parts."

She laughed again, but Drake could tell she was serious, and that the county sheriff was probably someone who did not mess around.

"But," Sella continued, the smile disappearing into a concerned look again, "Do you think it's safe for you to go see this cousin of Natalie's? If he's been involved and gets nervous about you connecting him to the crime, couldn't you be in danger?"

"Nah, I don't think so," He said, "He only knows me as the clueless schmo who was dumped by his cousin."

Sella winced at his frank assessment and instantly Drake felt bad for saying it and wished he could retract the words.

"Whoa, that didn't sound very forgiving, did it? See what I mean about bitterness? Sometimes, I'm reminded that I have a long way to go, God help me."

"I understand. Really, I do." Sella nodded, her brown eyes clouding slightly with a memory that Drake wasn't privy to and obviously was very painful for her.

Of course, Sella knew what he meant by being left by a spouse. How utterly thoughtless, callous, obtuse - *a bumbling idiot, that's what he was.*

As the moment stretched between them, the silence took on a life of its own. Normally comfortable with leading conversation, Drake was left devoid of words. How could he recover from such a mistake?

"I'm sorry, Sella, I wasn't thinking of anyone but myself," Without realizing what he was doing, Drake reached across the counter to grasp her fingers, "I'm sorry for saying anything that would bring back bad memories for you."

He smiled weakly, still berating himself in his mind, and glanced down at her fingers in his hand and then stared at them, as if shocked they were still there. She had beautiful fingers, long and delicate, and no wedding ring. Looking up hastily, he patted her on the back of her hand and stood up suddenly.

"I think I'd better go now. It's been a great day all around but I'm getting tired. Tell the guys thanks again for letting me tag along with them today. And thank you for dinner and the evening."

Sella pushed her chair back from the counter and stood next to him, her fresh, slightly flowery perfume filling his senses as she followed behind a few steps as he walked towards the front door.

"Yes, anytime. We had fun too." Sella leaned against the door with her hand on the door handle as he walked past her onto the front porch.

"Say, Drake?" She called out as he stepped onto the stone walkway leading to the driveway.

"Yeah?" Something in the middle of his chest did a turn when she called his name. He supposed it was his heart. It wasn't the first time today he'd noticed his heart reacting that way.

"You have my number. Call me when you get back from Duluth. I'd like to know things went okay for you."

He heard her request, but he had a hard time processing it because he was focused on how her ash-blonde hair floated perfectly around her face and down her neck and her eyes had that entrancing quality, almost like a cat.

"Oh, okay, sure," He had to say something or else she would notice him staring, so he blubbered, "I will let you know."

He lowered his head and began to walk again towards his car.

"And, Drake?" She called a second time, having stepped out further onto her porch. *There it was again. That flipping thing his heart was doing.*

"Yeah?" He asked, stepping a bit closer again so he wouldn't miss a word she said.

"What are your plans if you don't find out anything when you're in Duluth? Will you head back to Chicago?"

"I don't know. I'm only thinking ahead one day at a time, no real plan." It was the truth, but he felt like it was only partially true now. What *was* the plan in all this? *And what part did Sella play in it?*

Drake watched as she nodded and then sweeping her hair behind her ear again, she glanced down at the floor planks of the front porch.

Moved by her repose - the way she listened well and cared deeply – Drake realized how much he had come to enjoy spending these past few days in her presence. It didn't matter that he barely knew her, he was overcome with the need to tell her something about how he felt but he wasn't sure what it was he was feeling yet. All he knew was that he enjoyed her company and that he was grateful to God that he'd met her.

"Thanks, again, Sella. You've become a friend when I needed one and I appreciate that. I will let you know if anything interesting comes out of this trip to Duluth. Take care."

CHAPTER 12

2000 - 2003

Natalie

The years in Charlotte were really great. We found an apartment just off-campus and attended classes like other kids our age. I say kids because I wasn't even twenty and we were still full-time students, but already at that time, we understood that we were different than the people around us. We were older than them in mindset and much wiser to the ways of the world.

TC was now Anthony to everyone, and he reminded me constantly that TC was gone and that I was to call him Anthony. He grew a beard, cut his hair shorter and wore glasses instead of contacts. He took on a scholarly look and played the part of the nerdy graduate student.

His newest mark -that's what we'd call them - was a professor who had a penchant for on-line gambling and needed someone to make him quick cash in the stock market or other "high risk, high reward" investments.

TC was all over that and the professor was on the line right away, but of course, he didn't know it. The guy was so impressed with the talk, he even passed Anthony's name to some of his friends and the ponzi scheme was born.

I kept my real name but nothing else about me stayed the same. I kept a low profile while I perfected my new persona. It was during these early days in Charlotte where I realized the almost unlimited potential of being a woman, especially one with a soft, southern accent, big blue eyes, and silky blonde hair.

I took pride in the fact that I was not just "any" pretty woman. I became the kind of woman who would use my persona to get whatever I wanted. It was my game, my act; it became my profession.

At first, I challenged myself with insignificant things — get a guy to ask me out when I knew he had a girlfriend, get a professor to give me an A in his class without deserving it, get the internet guy to hook us up for free — and I would lure them along until I got what I wanted.

It was like a hunt — thrilling as I realized that it was working exactly as planned and then disappointing when it was over. That sense of disillusionment, almost a sense of loss, became a place that I hated. I avoided that hollow feeling by moving on to the next challenge.

I called it my sickness.

TC knew who I was and that I was sick like that. He said it wasn't a sickness, it was a gift. He encouraged me to expand my horizons, up the ante a little.

We started to hunt marks in bars all over the state. While TC watched me from across the room, I would con guys into buying me drinks and dinner and when they let their guard down, I would steal their wallets. One time, while the guy went to the restroom, we stole his car and left it three hours away, just for the fun of it.

Gradually, with TC's mentoring, I moved on to more in-depth scams that required me to work part time in an office of a small business, ingratiate myself to the boss/owner and then start to steal money. Sometimes it was just petty cash, sometimes it was padding invoices and taking home a cut of the bank deposits. I always kept it small and infrequent so they wouldn't notice. After I felt I'd accomplished the challenge, I would find a reason to quit, always on good terms. I even got a glowing recommendation from one of them, obviously they hadn't caught on to me.

During those years, we had a great life. I was doing well in classes, we had more than enough money and we had our "play life" at home. It was kind of like playing house.

TC was just doing what he did best: Taking people for a ride. There were moments that I lost track of his schemes because he was into so many. I fell more in love with him than I dreamed I ever could. He filled my days and nights with a sense of excitement, and I came really close to feeling alive again. Something I hadn't felt since I killed my stepfather all those years before.

One morning, it was the day before Christmas 2002, I woke up and realized that I was happy. Truly happy.

That was a great morning, that was a great feeling.

I was pregnant.

And that was the day that I was going to tell TC.

I hadn't questioned whether to keep the baby. It was TC's baby. Of course, we would make this a family, together.

All morning, I floated. I was in another world, trying to think of the best way to tell him. Finally, that afternoon as we were watching a football game on television, I left the room to get more chips and salsa and came back with a baby bottle stuck in the middle of the salsa bowl.

He stared at it for a long moment before he looked at me and said, "No."

I said, "What?"

I couldn't believe the look on his face.

"No." He stated again, his voice low and menacing.

"What do you mean No? It's too late for No. I'm pregnant and we're having a baby."

"That's what I mean. No. You may have decided to have a baby, but I am definitely not having a baby."

"Well, you can't just ignore it, TC. You're going to be father."

"I've told you a million times, I am not TC. And I'm never going to be a father. Never."

"Well, it's too late-"

"It's not too late. You can decide what you want to do with it, but I don't want anything to do with it. You hear me?"

"But-"

"I said No. If you want to keep it, you go right ahead. But I'm outta your life for good then because I don't want anything to do with a baby. You got that?"

He stood up, left the house and I didn't see him for two days. By the time he returned, I'd packed my bags and found an apartment of my own across town.

In those two days of pain, I forced myself to forget our play life and all the good times we'd shared. I forgot the idea of a family and I forgot that I'd ever loved him.

TC didn't exist anymore. He disappeared from my life.

And, eight months later, his baby boy didn't exist anymore either. I gave the baby up for adoption without ever seeing his little baby face.

I'm sure it was sweet, his little baby face. But, as soon as I got in the cab in the hospital parking lot that day, I forgot that I was a mom.

I say now that I hate men, but that's not always been true.

After hating men like my stepfather, when I met TC, I grew to believe one man was worth loving.

I was wrong. After our time in Charlotte, where I'd been used by a man that I loved, where I'd been deluded into thinking I really meant something to him, I finally understood the truth.

There is no such thing as a man worth loving, only those that are worth using.

CHAPTER 13

2019

Drake

The drive from Twin Shores to Duluth was postcard picturesque that afternoon and it was obvious the photography in the brochure he'd picked up in the Twin Cities hotel didn't do justice to the scenery. Mesmerizing in their beauty, the sun-dappled blue waters of Lake Superior travelled alongside the highway and would ebb away from rocky peaks and then be replaced by masses of trees blocking the views of the lake beyond, only to be interrupted again by low-lying, rocky beaches and small, sleepy lake towns. All the while, the sharp fishy smells of marine life and the subtle sting of northern pines mingled together on the breeze reminding Drake of summer vacations at his parents' lake cabin.

Even though the scenery was breathtaking at times, as he neared Duluth, Drake focused his mind on his line of questioning for Natalie's cousin Dane and he hoped that Dane would be cordial to him. Although it had been years since they'd seen each other, when Drake last spoke to him, they had been on friendly terms.

Natalie had introduced him as her favorite cousin, but from what Drake could tell, he was the only cousin she ever spoke to. Their connection went back to the time when Natalie and her parents

Allison and Jeff had moved from Atlanta to the Twin Cities, back in the 90s.

Although Natalie remembered the move from Georgia to Minnesota was a tough adjustment for a small child, she said that the closer proximity to Dane and his parents, who lived in Duluth, was the one bright spot.

Not long after the move, however, Natalie's father died from a rare form of blood cancer and it was obvious this traumatic period of her life left a deep mark on Natalie.

It took some time for her to share it with him, but finally Natalie had admitted that she'd never gotten over the death of her father and she blamed her mother for his death, even though, rationally, she knew he had died of the effects of the virulent cancer.

Drake could tell that the true reason for Natalie's resentment towards her mother was due to the speed with which she remarried. Within six months of Jeff's death, Allison remarried Clive Chisholm, the stepfather that Natalie never called by name. He was simply known as "that man."

The fact that her mother had remarried someone else so quickly felt like a complete betrayal, and even after he died from an untimely fall when she was fourteen, Natalie didn't have a kind word to say about her stepfather.

Although an accident like that would often bring families closer together, it worked the opposite with Natalie and Allison. Eventually, the resentment between them built to a point where Natalie moved out, lived with friends, and began to make her own way in life.

There were always holes in Natalie's life story that bothered Drake. Compared to his milk and cookies existence growing up on a farm in middle America with two parents and a sister, Natalie's life of independence and hard-fought survival seemed incredible and almost unbelievable.

Even though Drake was curious to learn more about her life, patterns emerged when Natalie's past life came up in conversation. Basically, she would shut down. It always became about how she wanted to move on, how she wasn't defined by the people of her past so why bother talking about them etc.

She would always tell him that today was what mattered, yesterday was over and she'd forgotten it already. When she'd say things like that, it never occurred to Drake that if she meant what she said, then it was just as likely that someday, *he* would be amongst the people she'd forget.

Drake switched off the ignition and took a deep breath as he glanced across the street at Dane's house with its crumbling curbing and scrabbled grass yard, enclosed with chain link fence.

Duluth was a unique town, built on a series of hills, with wide expanses of Lake Superior and its shipping port visible from many neighborhoods dotted up the hillsides. This particular neighborhood did not have a lake view, however, and its collection of faded and ramshackle two-story homes was in need of some serious repair. Unfortunately, it looked like the people who lived here were just too strapped for cash or were simply too tired to try.

Dane's house was a gray color reminiscent of a stormy Lake Superior sky, with darker gray shutters on the ground level windows and an American flag mounted on a peeling, once-white wood column that held up a sagging front porch.

In the shaded light of the wide front porch, Dane, dressed in a light blue twill uniform, sat in a camp chair with a bright green Igloo cooler on the floor next to his feet, his pet dog panting gently as he slept in a slanted ray of sunlight a few feet away.

Well, here goes − nothing. Drake finished the thought in his mind as he opened his car door and stepped resolutely across the street in the direction of the house.

Or it could be something, Drake. You never know.

"Hey, how are you, Dane? Been a long time, hasn't it?" Might as well try a confident tone, Drake thought and forced his mouth into a bright smile as he held his hand out towards the man who sat, still rooted in his chair.

"Sure has. Was surprised to hear from you, Drake." Dane started to stand up as he shook Drake's hand, but Drake waved him down again, "Well, welcome to Duluth, man. Take a seat - I got a Coke for ya', if you're interested."

"Sure, thanks, sounds good." Drake opened the tab of the can and motioned towards the sleeping dog in the corner, "He looks like a nice friend. Have you had him for a while?"

"Yeah, Mary got him from the shelter. Said he was there too long, and no one was coming to take 'im so we got 'im. He's named Rex." Dane's dog rolled open an eye at the sound of his name, as if he knew they were talking about him, then closed it again as if he could care less what they were saying.

"Yeah, I miss having a dog," Drake continued conversationally, it might help to warm Dane up, he thought. People always liked to talk about their pets, "We had a dog on the farm where I grew up. It's just so much harder having one in a city apartment and working like I do. Not enough time."

"Yeah. Still livin' in Chicago?" Dane bent towards the floor where he retrieved a lit cigarette from a cracked ceramic ashtray next to his foot.

"Yes, that's right, still there," Drake said, as he reminded himself that to get a little information, he would have to give a little information, "I have a business partner, been in business for many years now. I guess we're getting old." Drake took a swallow of the soda, then continued casually, "How about you, Dane? What line of work are you in now?" Drake sat down on the top wooden step, trying to ignore the peeling paint that was sticking to his jeans.

"Well, you know me, I've been in lots of things off and on. Some of them not always been the best of things. But the past few years I've turned myself around – got me a gig working as a delivery man. Driving truck, delivering bread and baked goods all around this area, stuff like that."

Even though he wanted to believe him whole-heartedly, Drake took the news of his redemption with a grain of salt. It would take more than a mere statement of regret for his past to convince Drake that Dane was innocent in this thing with Natalie.

But the truth was, the more he thought about it, the more he wanted to believe that Dane was innocent in all this. *He was her family. He couldn't have done something to hurt her, right?*

"That's great, Dane," Drake tried to keep his thoughts in order, and not reveal his doubts, "Glad to hear it."

"Yeah, when you and Nat were- well, last time we talked, I mean, you know I was going through some tough times. But I got my life straightened out now. Been sober for four years. Mary has been a life saver for me. You met Mary, remember?"

"Yes, I remember Mary," Drake remembered Dane's wife Mary as the quiet, soft-spoken type, but obviously, she held sway with Dane if she was able to influence his life in that way, "Is she here today?"

"No, she works PM shift at a retirement home. She said to say Hi to you."

"Okay, well, I'm sorry I won't see her. Tell her Hi from me too."

"Okay, I will." Dane paused, took a long drag from his cigarette and then rubbed the tops of his legs almost nervously before saying, "So, it's been like, a lot of years since I talked to you, Drake. All of a sudden, after Natalie shows up dead on the North Shore, I get a call from you and then you show up here, all the way from Chicago. Call me crazy, but I can't help but wonder why."

"Well, actually, I started out in Minneapolis. We have a business office there and I was in town with work." Drake paused, as he realized that, while it was true, it seemed like a weak excuse. It would probably produce better results if he just came out with the truth.

"So, you might think it's weird," Drake continued, "But I was just leaving Minneapolis for home, when I got the idea to come up here instead. For some reason, I had to see where Natalie died so I drove up to Twin Shores and went to the river where they found her car."

Drake paused and watched Dane's face as he absorbed his confession. He didn't seem nervous about what Drake might discover in Twin Shores but then, maybe he was a good actor. His cousin Natalie sure had the gift, it might run in the family.

Feeling a bit embarrassed about his honesty, and wanting to see how Dane would react to raw emotion about Natalie's death, Drake continued, "I know this all sounds morbid-"

"Yeah, kinda does sound weird," Dane's squint of disbelief sure looked authentic, "What did you expect to find there?"

That question set Drake on alert again as he tried to ascertain if Natalie's cousin was asking out of courtesy or if he was nervous about Drake asking too many questions that might entrap him into confessing to his part in this. But knowing that he needed more information, Drake soft-pedaled his reply.

"I didn't expect to find anything there and I don't really know why I went. You know, it's not really like me - doing rash things like that, going places without a plan."

"Yeah," Dane snorted in disbelief as he exhaled some smoke, "It does seem a bit odd to go all the way up there since she wasn't even married to you when she died."

"Yeah, I know. I guess part of me will always love her," Drake said it out loud and realized that he meant it. As he watched Dane react to the bold statement, Drake thought, *How's that for honesty?* And now that it was out in the open, he felt like he was on a roll as he continued, "Dane, did you ever meet Rolph Sartell?"

"No, Natalie never brought him around. But I know that he was old enough to be her father."

"That's true, he was." A few years ago, that blunt statement would have knifed him straight through. Now it just left Drake numb and a bit sad.

"Well, whatever rocks your boat," Dane continued, "I never could figure out Natalie's choice in men," As he realized what he said, Dane cleared his throat slightly and smiled sheepishly at Drake, "No offense-"

"None taken," Drake waved the insult away with his hand, "But, now I gotta ask, what do you mean 'Natalie's choice in men?'"

"Well, she was just ... well, I mean she was just all over the board with guys. Some young, some old, some good lookin', some uglier than the day is long."

Here was his opening and Drake leapt on it.

"But ... they all had money, didn't they?" He said it quietly, but also very deliberately. Just to make sure Dane heard every word.

He looked up suddenly, as if shocked by the stark truth being spoken so bluntly.

"Yeeahh, they did." Dane dropped his gaze and looked at the Coca Cola can he held in his hands, "She couldn't help it. Natalie collected men like that."

"Yeah, it seems that she did," Drake agreed noncommittally and paused for a moment before asking, "Dane, did Natalie ever tell you anything about her marriage to Rolph?"

"Yeah, we talked. But she never said much about him. Why? The guy wasn't hurting her, was he?" Dane's eyes closed into slits and lit up defensively.

"No, not that I know of," Drake reassured him quickly, "I was just wondering about the other stuff that was going on– the stuff with his business."

"Oh, you mean her stealing from him." His body relaxed again as Dane leaned back in his chair and took a drag from his cigarette, waiting for Drake to show his hand.

"Yeah, that. Did she ever tell you she was doing anything like that?"

"No, but I'm not surprised. Natalie's view of right and wrong was always a little on the gray side. The only thing that mattered to her was Natalie. It didn't hurt that she was gorgeous and wicked smart either. She could get guys to do whatever she wanted."

Boy, was that an understatement, Drake thought.

"But," Drake continued to press, "Did she ever tell you that she'd done something like this before?"

"Ahh, I'm not sure I know what you mean–" Dane sat forward again in his chair, his legs tensing and his mouth turning down into a firm line.

"Come on, Dane, you know what I mean. Did she con other guys out of money?" The words came out more combative than Drake wanted but once they were out, it was too late to change course.

"Well, you should know, you were married to her." Dane shot back.

"But, that's the point," Frustrated, Drake's voice rose as he shook his head in confusion, "I *was* married to her and I *don't* know. You have to see how that's bugging me, right?"

"I just don't know why you'd ask now. Did she steal from you too?" Dane questioned.

"No. Everyone asks me that now that she's gone, but no, she didn't steal from me." Drake took a deep breath and met Dane's eyes squarely, ready to ask the difficult question, "But I just wonder why - if my wife was a serial con-woman - why didn't any of you ever say anything to me?"

There the accusation was out. See what he has to say to that.

"Ex-wife, Drake," Dane countered in self-defense, "She was your ex-wife-"

"Okay, whatever, *ex*-wife," Drake interrupted, "Still, why didn't anyone ever let me know she was into this kind of thing? Were you all complicit in it? Maybe you were just waiting for her to rip me off too?"

"Wait-" A light went on in Dane's eyes, "After what I just told you that I'm staying clean and outta trouble, you still think I'm involved in Natalie's cons?"

Dane grunted in disgust and rose from his chair to stand over Drake, rousing the dog Rex to stand at attention in the corner, "Say it, Drake. You think that I'm involved and that's why you really came up here, to try to get me to confess to something that I had no part of-"

"No, that's not true," Drake rose from his seat on the step and stood his ground, forcing his voice into a controlled pattern, "I really did come up here to see where she died but I got thinking, why was she in Minnesota in the first place? She hardly ever spoke to her mother and you're the only other connection that I could think of."

As he finished speaking, Drake took a deep breath and tried to slow down the racing inside his chest. And while Dane turn his back and lit another cigarette, he reviewed his options. If Dane wasn't involved, maybe he would have some ideas on why Natalie was here. It wouldn't do any good to anger him so much that he didn't want to help.

"Listen, Dane," Drake entreated to his turned back, "I know this is coming off that I am suspicious of you, but I'm really just trying to figure some things out. If I'm wondering about why she died here, I'm sure the police are too."

"Oh, the police – so now you're trying to *threaten* me because of my past?" With his body half-turned, Dane spat the words towards the floor, not meeting Drake's eyes.

"No, of course not-"

"Good," He looked up and pinned Drake to the wall with his words, "'cause that would be really rich, coming from the guy they figured for her disappearance in the first place."

"Exactly," Drake agreed, surprising himself and Dane with the honest acknowledgement, "I know how it feels for them to breathe down your neck when you're innocent. Trust me, it's not pleasant. So, can you help me try to figure out why she was here? Do you know anyone else that she had a connection to in Minnesota?"

Slowly, Dane's demeanor eased into something akin to cordial as he suggested, "Well, maybe she was just driving through on her way somewhere else or maybe she was heading somewhere to lay low for a while, I dunno. Maybe it's just a coincidence that she was up here."

"I've thought of those things too," Happy to be less contentious and back in mystery-solving mode, Drake said, "But, of all the places she could go, why here? And why was her car found in a river? And if someone double-crossed her and tried to get rid of her, why did she still have all that cash with her in the car?"

He leaned forward again with his questions, his hands slicing the air for emphasis.

"I don't know, Drake," Dane backed away from his intensity and continued, "but I can tell you that none of us – her family – is involved. And, just so you know, I talked to her mom Allison at the funeral. She's as confused as me about Natalie and what was happening with her at the time of her death."

Defeated again, Drake rubbed his suddenly burning sore eyes as the clouds around her death darkened even further in confusion and mystery.

"Okay, okay," Drake sighed in exhaustion, "I guess that's all there is then. No one will ever know what happened. We just have to let the detectives do their job."

"But do you think they will come after me?" Dane spoke up nervously, drawing on his cigarette again.

"Honestly, I don't know, Dane. I'm not sure where they're looking – or if they're looking."

"Not looking? You mean 'cause the police don't think she's worth their time?"

"No, I'm not saying that exactly. I'm just saying if I'm them and I have the victim in jail with his own set of crimes and the perpetrator's dead - found with the stolen cash, no less - I'd be hard pressed to find a reason to pursue this much further."

"But if she was murdered, they sure should be looking into it." Dane said as Rex sauntered over and sat next to him, pressing his head against Dane's knee.

"We don't know how she died. The authorities think it's an accident from what I've heard," Drake shared noncommittally, "But listen, what do I know - I'm just questioning the how's and the why's. I don't think we will know exactly how or why she died until we find out if she was pulling this con alone or with someone else."

"Oh boy, this is a mess," Dane reached down and patted Rex behind the ears before he looked up again and asked, "Did you ask Allison if she knew of anyone? I know Natalie had a lot of guys over the years. Maybe one of them was involved?"

"I've already asked her, and Allison couldn't really think of anyone specifically."

"Hmmm," Dane closed his eyes, deep in thought, as he knelt near the dog, "There is one person that comes to mind. He's a guy from way, way back in her past though, unlikely that they kept in touch. He lives on the Range, back with his family now that he's out of prison. In Hibbing, I think." Dane looked up with one eye closed in a squint against the setting sunlight coming in from under the porch roof.

"What's the guy's name?"

"Jack Dawson. He dated Natalie when she roomed with me here in Duluth. He was a friend of mine at the time – but he's bad news. I wish I'd never introduced them," Dane shook his head as he continued his recollection.

"What kind of bad news?"

"Drugs-and-stolen-cars kind of bad news." He stood again with his statement and moved his leg away from the dog that was leaning heavily against it in hopes of more attention.

"Okay-" Drake swallowed hard, just another example of his delicate, sweet-mannered wife being a complete act. If he was going to continue to push this, he'd better develop a thick skin – he was bound to hear a lot more where this came from, "And, Natalie dated him?"

"Well, yeah, eventually she moved in with him. It surprised me at first, I didn't really think he was her type. She seemed too classy for him, but as soon as she saw the money he flashed around, I could tell she was interested."

"So, how involved was she in his – business?"

"From what I saw, she was very involved. That's why he was so pissed at her when things went south."

"Things went south-" Drake frowned, waiting for the other shoe to drop.

"Yeah, Jack thought he was a big shot, kept expanding his 'territory' all over the north country, all the small towns and the larger ones too. He got so busy that eventually, he wanted someone smart to keep track of the money - someone that he could trust and that no one would suspect was involved – someone like college grad, good-girl Natalie."

"And, then things went south-" Drake reminded him where he left off.

"Yeah, she stuck the screws to him – skimmed beaucoup thousands, then turned him in to the cops. Well, that's what Jack thought at the time 'cause around then she started dating a DEA agent-"

"No. Way." Drake's brain felt like it was spinning straight out of his skull and he leaned back against the porch column for support.

"Yeah, but no one could prove any of that. The part of her ratting him out to the Feds, I mean. The DEA agent was from the Twin Cities, and he was married, they weren't together for long-"

"Oh, my gosh." Drake let the outlandish, impossible tale settle in for a long moment as he desperately tried to gather all the loose ends together.

So, it was true. He hadn't known his wife at all. She had been a complete and utter stranger to him. A phantom. A figment of his imagination. A woman without a past, present only in the moment she shared with him. A woman completely different before he met her and completely different after she left him.

Knowing this, what did it say about the time when Natalie was with him?

As he drove away from Dane's house a few minutes later, convinced that her cousin had not been involved in the con, Drake asked himself the question again:

What did all this reveal about the time when Natalie was with him?

And in his car alone, he had the courage to answer it:

His wife and his marriage had been a figment of his imagination. All of it. Fake.

Paused at a stop sign on his way down the hill towards downtown Duluth, Drake gazed over the hood of his car at the gray blue waters of Lake Superior that seemed to stretch forever, no end in sight.

If he could just fly away over that water, be free of all this, be alive again. If only.

His phone beeped with a text on the seat beside him and the Bluetooth lit up on his dash with a message from Dan in the Minneapolis office. Just confirming that they were still planning to review his new customer proposal in an hour.

How could he focus on something so real-world like work when he was currently residing in a dream-world, an alternate reality, like this?

Drake worked his fingers over his temples and across his forehead trying to make the spinning stop. He had to do something. He must take action to make it stop.

Jabbing mercilessly at the dash, he dialed the number for his ex-mother-in-law and pulled into traffic again, continuing north and east out of town. Back towards Twin Shores.

"Hello, Drake." Her soft voice permeated the interior of the car like a warm, fleece blanket. But he couldn't allow that sweet voice to sidetrack him. He was on a mission and he steadied himself to say what he had to say in a voice that reflected exactly how he felt.

"Allison, I've just been to Dane's where he shared with me some 'pleasant' memories of my ex-wife's storied past. Now, I know you don't think you owe me any information about Natalie, but I want you to tell me whatever you know because this whole thing is really starting to stink and I know the cops would be very interested in some of these tidbits that you all conveniently forgot to mention to me over the years."

His outburst was met with silence and her hesitation spoke volumes; he must have shocked her southern sensibilities straight off the back porch. But she was a steely one, his ex-mother-in-law. He had to give her that.

"Well, I'm sure I don't know what you're talkin' about, Drake." She paused just long enough for Drake to feel the heat of anger burn from under his shirt and burst onto his neck and face as she continued smoothly, "As you know, Natalie and I did not have a close relationship-"

"Save it, Allison. I'm done with that," Drake interrupted fiercely, "You need to tell me about these other people that were involved with Natalie over the years. Already, I'm going to look into this drug dealer former boyfriend of hers that's now *out of prison*. He sounds like a real upstanding citizen."

"Well, I don't know anythin'-"

"Forgive me for doubting that, Allison. It just strikes me as crazy that when I ask you about people she's known – people who might wish her harm – that you wouldn't think to mention this guy. Makes me wonder who else is out there that you've *forgotten* to mention."

"Drake, I don't appreciate your tone," Allison clucked into the phone, her voice edged with sarcasm and laced with a low-boil anger, proof that she was done playing nice with him, "I think it should be mighty clear to you by now, but because you seem hell-bent on nosin' your way 'round this affair, I will state it more plainly for you."

For dramatic effect, Allison paused again, and Drake flipped the air conditioning vents to blow directly onto his heated face to avoid sweating.

He didn't care that she was mad at him. Maybe it took him pushing her this far to get a rise out of her – finally, maybe she would give him a lead on who was involved in this, he thought as he waited for her to continue.

"Natalie had secrets, Drake," Allison continued in a low, heavy drawl, "She had lots of 'em, goin' way back. But secrets are just that – you ain't s'pose to talk 'bout them, or they won't be secrets anymore – and people get hurt. You understan' what I'm sayin'? You won't get her secrets outta her momma, that's for sho'. And don't call here agin'. If I see your number, I won't pick up."

Click.

CHAPTER 14

2019

Sella

"Awe, Poppy, you can't make that shot, don't even try!" Henri teased Luca as he watched his grandfather eye a difficult shot on the pool table.

"You don't think so, huh? Well, let's see about that!"

Chuckling, Luca bent low over the side of the table and slid his pool cue deftly across his fingers expertly sending the ball into the side pocket, while bouncing one of Henri's color safely out of range.

"Ha! There you go, watch and learn, young man, watch and learn!" Poppy boasted as he stood up victoriously, their second game tonight completed.

Many nights they passed the time playing pool in the garage-turned-mancave. Always enjoying the banter between them, Sella would often sit out there to read or do office paperwork.

This evening, she was surrounded by unmatched socks, doing her best to find mates from amongst the stacks that she'd sorted by color.

"You want one more game to earn back some respect, Henri?" Luca asked as he set balls into the triangle.

"Sure! But I gotta go get something to drink first. You want anything, Poppy?" As he scaled the few steps towards the kitchen, Henri slowed slightly to wait for the answer.

"No, I'm okay." Luca smiled at his grandson as he joined Sella on the couch, "Better ask your mother if she'd like anything."

"Yeah, sorry. Mom?"

"No, thanks, Henri. But, just water for you, okay? No juice before bed." Sella answered, finally locating a blue and red striped sock that had been evading her for the past fifteen minutes.

A few minutes later, when Henri still hadn't returned, Sella called out to him, wondering what could be taking him so long. When there was no reply, she stood up to check things out and stopped short of the steps when she heard a voice of a man – the subtle, low tones of which she now recognized as Drake Connor's voice – coming within earshot from the kitchen beyond.

She waited, a few unmatched socks still in her hands, as he filled the doorway a few feet from her. Without thinking, Sella pulled a few wayward hairs behind her ears and smiled up at him like a shy teenager.

She'd gotten a text from Drake two days ago. He relayed that his trip to Duluth went fine but the cousin wasn't involved in Natalie's disappearance and she hadn't heard from Drake since. Given this, she half expected to never hear from him again, so she was surprised to find him show up at their house unannounced.

Sella didn't like surprises. Maybe that explained why her heart was beating faster than normal and her face felt warm. In fact, *she really disliked surprises.*

"Hello! I hope I'm not interrupting anything," Drake's voice and intense presence filled the room as he joined them, "Henri said you were just starting another pool game. He told me you weren't going easy on him, Luca." Drake joked as he set a hand on Luca's shoulder.

"Ha, ha, no, I guess not–" Luca laughed, the uncertainty in his eyes giving away the fact that he couldn't remember who Drake was.

"Dad, this is Drake," Sella interjected calmly, at the same time, trying to smooth her voice into a more welcoming tone, "Remember that day when we took him fishing with us and then you and Henri stayed over at Phillip's house and you had a campfire?"

"Oh. Yes. Well, maybe I remember that. I have troubles with my memory, see?" Luca explained to Drake as if it was the most normal thing in the world to forget something that happened less than a week ago.

"Ah, sure, no problem, Luca," Drake agreed amicably and squeezed her father's shoulder warmly before dropping his hand, "We had fun and caught some fish, that's what's important."

"Yeah, and boy were they good!" Henri spoke up from the steps behind Drake, water glass in hand.

"Yes, they sure were," Drake said, obviously a nod to their fish dinner together the other night. As he met her eyes he apologized, "Sorry to just drop in on you guys. I was hiking a few miles from here and thought I'd take the chance you were home."

"That's okay," Sella said with a smile, but it felt stiff on her face. Why should he want to stop in at all? For no good reason, it made her feel a little uneasy. Or, was a better word *unsteady*?

"Did you have a nice hike?" Sella continued, trying her best to be polite.

"Yes, I did. I started up the Superior Hiking Trail and turned around again, even though I would have liked to keep going to Gooseberry Falls if I had time. Everything was so beautiful and peaceful."

"Sella likes to hike. She could show you some really nice places," Luca spoke up as he finished setting the pool table for the next game, "You should show your friend some hikes around Silver Bay sometime, Sella. He'd really like that."

From behind Drake, Henri grabbed a pool cue and waited politely for Drake to move aside so he could join Luca at the table. As she observed his reaction, Drake's eyes crinkled into a grin.

"That would be fun. Maybe I can convince her to do that sometime." Drake was speaking to Luca, but he was watching her face. Not sure if he was teasing or serious, Sella turned back to her laundry basket with its kaleidoscopic assortment of socks and pulled it into her arms.

"Yeah, maybe sometime. There are gorgeous hikes all around here." She replied.

Because there wasn't another explanation for his visit, Sella concluded that Drake must want to talk about his visit to Duluth out of earshot of the other two, so she offered, "I'm taking these socks upstairs. Drake, do you want to come with me and tell me about your visit to Duluth?"

"Sure," He readily agreed, confirming her assumption, "See you two later. Take it easy on your grandpa, Henri."

"Nah, Poppy always wins, he's really good at pool. But this might be the time I beat you, Poppy."

"Well, let's see about that-" Luca said as he reached for his pool cue.

It was obvious they would forget about Sella and Drake as soon as they left the room.

Because she wanted to enjoy the waning warmth of the sunset, Sella suggested the front porch for their conversation. As she sat down on the top step, she leaned back against the knobby surface of a rock column and motioned for Drake to join her on the opposite side of the step.

"So, your trip didn't get you any closer to knowing why Natalie was in Minnesota?" She asked immediately, because obviously he wasn't here for small talk.

A startled expression passed over his tan face, almost as if he was surprised by how directly she asked. Or, maybe it was her tone of voice. Sella consciously tried to soften her perspective on this impromptu visit.

Give the guy a chance, Sella, she mentally scolded herself. He's a human being, after all, and he as much as told you that he was still in love with his ex-wife. Of course, he would want to figure out the circumstances surrounding her death.

"Well, no, not really," Drake said, his usually direct gaze now focused on his shoes or the string of ants that were marching along the flagstone path below them, "According to her cousin Dane, she wasn't here to see him or her mother, or any other family in the area from what he knew."

"And you believe him?"

"Yes, I do." Drake paused as a look passed across his face and he raised his intense, silver-glinted gaze towards her.

Was she mistaken, or did he seem extra "on-edge" tonight? She didn't know him well, and he always seemed to have a tightly-wound demeanor, but tonight his whole body seemed tense and his eyes had a force behind them that she didn't remember in her few encounters with him.

"He did give me some rather interesting information though," Drake continued, his voice firm and steady, "I've been wondering if you would be willing to help me out with it."

"Me?" Not at all what she expected, Sella uttered, "What can I do to help?"

"Dane told me that years ago, Natalie had a relationship with a guy from Hibbing and he thinks the guy still lives there." Drake took a deep breath before leaning closer to her, causing some of the hairs on the back of neck to raise, "Listen, I know none of this concerns you, Sella, and I don't really expect you to care about it, but it has been nice to be able to talk to someone about it. You have been a great support and it's really helped me."

"Okay," His body language and his words were so disparate, it was hard to assimilate both at the same time, "but you haven't told me what I can do to help."

"Well, here's the deal – I am planning to go to Hibbing to meet this guy. You said that you have a store location in Hibbing and a brother who lives there, right?" He raised his trim eyebrows with his plea.

"Yeah–" Before he even asked, Sella was almost positive he would convince her to do what he wanted. This was why he was successful in business; she was sure of it. He made it almost impossible to say no to him.

"Well, I was wondering if you would go there with me, kind of help me sleuth this thing a little. You could see if your brother knows the guy or knows anything about him. I would go find him by myself, I wouldn't ask you to be involved in anything dangerous–"

"You think the guy's dangerous?" She interrupted, re-thinking her position of only a moment ago. Dangerous was something she wanted no part of.

"That's the thing. I don't know. Years ago, he was into selling drugs and who knows what else. According to Dane, Natalie got wrapped up in all that and then ended up stealing some of the guy's money. It ended with the guy going to jail."

"What? Oh my gosh–" Without realizing, she raised her fingers to her mouth in surprise at the depth of illegality of it all.

"And that's not all. The rumor was that Natalie ratted him out to the DEA." He continued the outrageous tale, moving even closer to her with each sentence, almost as if he didn't want anyone else to hear.

"Really?"

"Yeah, but the rumors don't stop there. Turns out that while she was ratting out her drug dealer boyfriend, people say that she was having an affair with the married DEA agent on the case."

Sella wouldn't have been surprised if there was even more to the story, but he seemed to have exhausted the most shocking details because he sighed and his shoulders rounded slightly as he sat back against the rock column behind him.

"Oh, Drake. You've got to be kidding, this is too much-" Sella dropped her hand to her lap and looked out over the front yard at the peaceful expanse that was her life and thought, *wow, I live in a bubble.*

"I know," Drake spoke quietly, the energy sapped from his voice, "Tell me about it. I've spent the past two days praying about it - just trying to wrap my head around it. Now that I've said it all out loud, I realize that I'm not there yet."

"Oh, my gosh, I feel for you."

"Yeah. It's like an onion, each layer I take off, I think I'm getting somewhere but I find another layer and then another layer. Each is more pungent than the last."

"Mhmm." Contemplating his dilemma, Sella nodded, her brows knit into a frown, as she tried to sort through all the details of what he'd just told her.

"You have no reason to get involved, Sella," Drake spoke again into the silence of the woods at dusk as he looked at her from the safe distance across the steps, "and you probably think I'm crazy for asking in the first place. I sure wouldn't blame you if you said no."

Drake dropped his gaze then, giving her a reprieve from its burning intensity and his difficult request.

Pausing cautiously before answering him, Sella wondered what her next words should be. Part of her – the protective mom and daughter – didn't want to get involved. She had way too much to lose if somehow this blew back on her family.

The other part of her wanted to help her new friend in some small way.

There had been moments in her life when Sella thought really hard about the consequences of her actions. And there were moments where she didn't think hard at all. Some of her more spontaneous moves, like her decision to marry Garrett without giving the relationship time to develop, were moments that she wished had worked out differently, and maybe if she'd thought about them harder, she would have made a few different choices.

But where would she be if she had? She might not be here, able to take care of her father, and she wouldn't have Henri.

Life was a series of choices. Sometimes you just couldn't think too hard about what came next.

Sella reached out across the safe space between them and patted Drake's forearm where it draped across his raised knee. Glancing up sharply, she could see he was startled by her touch and it made her smile.

"What day were you thinking you wanted to go to Hibbing?"

CHAPTER 15

2003 – 2006– 2009

Natalie

After I gave our baby away, I left Charlotte, determined to make it on my own, far away from TC. But a life of crime isn't as glamorous as they make it out to be in the movies. There are many days of tedious planning like where to live, what to do to earn steady cash, how to cover your tracks.

My plan was to work my way back to Minnesota. I took some cheap shots along the way, hustling some older men who were tempted by a "pretty young thing with a sharp head on her shoulders," and before I knew it, a few years had gone by.

TC had ended up living in Minnesota and called me occasionally over those years, usually using a different name and with a different cover story. Sometimes he'd bring me into his schemes, other times he'd keep them to himself. He kept things between mostly professional at that point. He acted like nothing had happened between us in Charlotte, so I did too.

Eventually, I made it back to Minnesota and lived with my cousin Dane while I finished my accounting degree at the U of M, Duluth so I could look legit on a resume.

While there, desperately needing money, I started lifting stuff right away, selling it on the internet, just to get by as I prospected my next mark.

It really was very tedious work, flirting with men all the time at hotel bars, casinos, coffee shops. Sometimes it took hours to get just a snippet of information that I could use.

But when I found that morsel, I was all over it and it's like the guy would bounce up and down with his hand in the air saying, "Oh, oh, pick me! Pick me!"

It wasn't random, trust me. I had learned from TC what to look for – the dirtier the person, the better the mark.

That's how it was with Cousin Dane's friend Jack, drug dealer to the North Shore and beyond. It was easy, almost too easy. I became Jack's girlfriend and then his "bookkeeper" - a position that had poor benefits but paid extremely well.

Then, it all got complicated real fast.

CHAPTER 16

2019

Drake

Even though he'd grown up in Minnesota, Drake had never visited this particular portion of the north country. That morning, as he and Sella neared the Iron Range – known as "The Range" to locals – signs of human life began to emerge again from the deep forest they had been in for the past hour. They passed mining sites abuzz with activity and through communities that felt typical to most Midwest small towns, much like the small farm town he grew up in. And, like his hometown, it was obvious these towns were working towns, focused on local industry – his hometown industry was agriculture, in these towns, the industry that drove the economies for generations had been mining.

Sella told him stories of the area, once known for its abundant iron ore, and the effects of the downturn over the past few decades. They mined taconite on a smaller scale now and there was talk of copper-nickel mining. She said that the people here were "scrappy" and had persevered through the toughest of times and the ones that had held on were likely some of the strongest people you'd ever meet.

Her description of the people and the area made Drake wonder whatever would draw Natalie to this part of the state. As he glanced out the window at the nondescript buildings and the mined ground with its layers of red, brown and gold ground, Drake was trying his best to envision Natalie, with her perfectly polished nails and her designer shoes, fitting into this community. The nearest Macy's had to be nearly 200 miles from here.

But, he reminded himself, he had to stop thinking of the Natalie that he'd met in Chicago and eventually fell in love with. As was becoming abundantly clear, that hadn't been the real Natalie at all. Somewhere in her past, she had lived here on the iron range and had convinced them all that this was where she belonged.

A lie, of course, but they had believed it. Her whole life, full of lies.

Now, Sella?

She was a different story.

He glanced across the seat towards her, dressed casually in a flannel top and dark jeans, as he half-listened to the cell phone conversation she was having with someone in her office.

A strikingly beautiful woman, intelligent and kind, Sella wasn't superficial in the least. That's not to say, she was the most outwardly friendly and conversational of people. Instead, she was one of those people that simply preferred to stay out of the spotlight.

It was becoming obvious to Drake as he spent more time with her, that she intentionally diverted conversation away from herself and instead steered the conversation towards others. She was a good listener, and it was easy to share so much with her that you found at the end of it, she hadn't shared anything about herself. It was obvious that she seemed most comfortable with that.

He was starting to realize that Sella placed people on a trust scale, probably a result of the unexpected demise of her marriage. On Sella's trust scale, the higher you rose, the more she would share.

It had started as a seed inside him a few days ago as he noticed the attraction he felt towards her, and he had prayed about it, but Drake was finding a nagging disappointment that he wouldn't be around long enough to reach a level of trust with her where she would share anything meaningful with him.

Always someone who worked on a schedule, in his mind, today was the last effort he would make to dig any further into Natalie's secret life. If nothing came of today, then so be it. He would move on. His life was in Chicago.

"Turn right at the stop light ahead. The shop is two blocks down." Sella closed out of her conversation and swiped through some emails on her phone, "Sebastian said that he has a few minutes before he has to leave for an appointment."

"Great. Will you be working at the store this morning?"

"Yes, I have to work out an issue with our POS system while I'm here. He's been complaining for a week about an error that keeps coming up for him on his tills," She smiled as she dropped her cell phone into the front pocket of her work bag, "So, you actually saved me a trip and it's been nice having company on this long drive for a change."

"I'm glad," Drake smiled at her generous statement, "Did you mention anything to your brother about me and why I'm with you today?"

"Ah, not specifically," Sella placed her aviator sunglasses over her eyes and glanced out the window, "He can get a little protective and he's kind of the suspicious type. It's best to let me explain it to him in person. He might not even know the guy you're looking for."

"Of course. I understand. If he doesn't know Jack Dawson, I will just ask around town. No big deal."

"But it is a big deal to you, Drake. Otherwise you wouldn't still be in Minnesota."

"Well, yeah, I guess you're right," Drake said as he pulled into a parking spot in front of the store, "But, I want you to know, Sella, that if nothing turns up today, that's it. I'm done looking."

"Okay, whatever you think." She smiled a half-smile and reached for the door handle.

Sebastian Lafayette was a lanky man, with fair skin and lively, dark eyes like Sella's. He glanced up from behind the counter as the bell on the front door announced their entrance, a slightly confused expression in his eyes.

"Good morning, Gisella! Long time, no see."

Never having heard her full name before, Drake was pleasantly surprised at how beautiful it sounded: Ji-zel -la.

It fit her perfectly, and he resolved in his mind that he would call her that from now on.

"Hello, brother," She called out to him, "How are things here in Hibbing?"

"Good, things are good," Sebastian closed the open till drawer in front of him, gathered some receipts from the counter and placed a stapler on top of them neatly, while he glanced over Sella's shoulder at Drake standing behind her, "You brought a guest?"

"Yes, this is Drake Connor. He's been staying in Twin Shores and is looking for some information on someone you might know from town."

"Hello, nice to meet you," Drake said as he stepped forward and shook the man's large hand, "You gave a great family, they've all been so hospitable."

"Oh, so you must be the guy that Dad was talking about the other night when I called," Sebastian's face crinkled into a grin as he glanced at his sister with a laugh, "Dad said that you were outside with a strange man. It's been a while since Gisella has had a stranger-"

"Okay, Sebastian, that's enough," Gisella interrupted brusquely, "Drake has some questions for you and I have some work to do before you leave to pick up that truck," Sella turned towards Drake with her eyebrows raised and a hurry-up look in her eyes, "What did you think Sebastian could help you with, Drake?"

"Yes. Well, I'm sure you know about the car wreck that your nephew Henri found in the river near their home last spring. The woman in the car was – well, she was my ex-wife. She had gone missing a few years ago and no one can quite figure out why she was in Minnesota. I've come out here to try to reconstruct a few things, try to figure out who she might know here. Gisella-" Sella glanced up at him in surprise at the use of her name but he continued as if nothing was out of the ordinary, "has been a great help to me as I've been trying to do this since I'm from Chicago and don't know anyone in the area."

"Hmm," Sebastian murmured an acknowledgement as if to say he was listening but didn't really have anything to add. Taking it as encouragement to elaborate, Drake continued.

"It turns out that Natalie – that's my ex-wife's name – had a connection to a guy who was from Hibbing and he may still live here. Do you know Jack Dawson?"

Sebastian blinked hard and snorted disapprovingly.

"Your ex-wife from Chicago knew Jack Dawson?"

"Yes, that's what I'm told," Drake continued, determined to proceed no matter what was revealed, no matter how bad it was, "Do you know him?"

"Yeah, I know him. Everyone around here knows him," Sebastian glanced at his sister with a confused stare, as if he was wondering how she could be mixed up in something so unsavory as this, "He's not – well, from what I know of him, he's alright now but he's got a past that's not lily-white, let's say."

"So, he still lives in Hibbing?"

"Yeah, he runs a rental business across town. He took it over from his parents a few years ago," Sebastian paused as if to make a point and his frown deepened before continuing, "After he got out of prison."

"Okay, great. I will go see him. What's the business named?"

"It's real creative – Dawson Rentals. It's on the highway going west out of town, you can't miss it."

"Okay. Great."

Drake glanced at Sella to see if she had anything to add but she just grinned back at him, as if she was glad for the news that Dawson was still in town then dropped the smile when she encountered her brother's bewildered gaze shifting between them.

"Well, okay then," Drake responded confidently, thrilled that he might find some answers, "Thanks for your help, Sebastian. I will check it out and I'll be back to pick you up later, Gisella."

Turning, Drake hurried out the door before he would be forced to answer any further questions about his ex-wife from the suspicious, protective brother of his new friend with the beautiful name.

"He's out back taking in a rental. You can go out there if you want," The teenage boy with multiple piercings running along his right ear mumbled before turning his attention back to the snowboarding video that was playing on the computer screen in front of him. *Man, that had to hurt,* Drake thought as he found himself staring at the series of earrings.

"Okay, thanks," Drake turned away and zigzagged past assorted paint sprayers, ceramic tile saws and small gas generators towards the door that stood propped open at the back of the store.

Once outside, he scanned the parking lot until he saw the man with the clipboard in his hand standing next to an older man and a moving van.

Drake waited in the shadows of the building as he watched the older man sign the paperwork, hand back the clipboard and then drive away in his SUV.

Jack Dawson had a weathered, hard-knock-life look about him. Heavy-set and not very tall, he had wispy-thin, dark hair and ruddy, red cheeks. As he squatted alongside the van, he checked the tires and seemingly satisfied, eventually he rose slowly and drew a lighter and a pack of cigarettes from the front pocket of his Dawson Rentals knit work shirt.

Leaning against the side panel, Jack Dawson took a drag on his cigarette and happened to glance towards the back door of the store where Drake was standing. His face registered surprise as he pulled the cigarette down and pushed himself away from the van and stood straight.

Wait a minute, Drake faltered. Was that a look of recognition? It never occurred to him that anyone would know him here in Minnesota.

But, maybe that was to his advantage, Drake thought as he crossed the parking lot towards the man. Maybe the guy would be more truthful if he suspected Drake was the kind of guy who would be involved in a crime and disappearance of a person. It might not hurt if he was a little intimated.

"Jack Dawson?"

"Yeah, that's me." With a bit of bravado, Jack placed his hands on his hips, the cigarette dangling from one of them.

"Drake Connor." Drake had reached him now but didn't bother to offer his hand for a handshake. The guy was definitely not receptive.

"I know who you are, I've seen your picture." Dawson's voice was raspy and hard-edged, like his demeanor.

"Okay. So, you know that I was married to Natalie a few years before she disappeared?"

"I know they thought you were involved in her disappearance." He sneered as he took a long drag from his cigarette.

"You're right, they did. But if you've kept up on the news, you also know that they formally cleared me after they found her in the river near Twin Shores."

"Yeah, I guess I heard that." He conceded, almost regretfully, Drake thought. This guy was really rubbing him the wrong way.

"And you probably know that she was on the run after stealing from her husband's business at the time of her death-" Drake paused, his sunglasses likely hid the disdain in his eyes, but he was sure it was evident in his voice and all over his face, "Did you know that too, Jack?"

"Yeah, I read that she had jacked the guy. Didn't surprise me." Jack Dawson took a drag from his cigarette and squinted through the smoke, "Why are you here, asking me these questions? I haven't had anything to do with Natalie in years."

"I wonder about that," Drake's suspicions heightened the longer he looked at Jack Dawson, "You seem to be very aware of her and the people in her life. Most people I've met in Minnesota don't have a clue of who I am, but you knew right away. Why is that?"

"Like I said, I watch the news."

"Okay," Drake took a deep breath and decided a new tact might work better, "But if you haven't been in touch with her for years, why would you be so interested in her life at all?"

"I don't know, curiosity I guess." Jack shrugged.

"You mean after they found her car last spring?"

"No," Jack admitted, and leaned against the van again, "I've wondered what happened to her since she disappeared. I heard about that and wondered who might have gotten to her."

"Why would you wonder if someone was out to get her?"

"Because she was that type of girl, duh. In her line of work, she made enemies."

"Work?"

"Man, are you that dumb or just playin' that dumb?" Jack snorted and blew a line of smoke towards Drake, "Cons. She was into conning people."

"Did she con you, Jack?" Drake asked, leaning in ever so slightly towards the man.

"Since you've showed up here, it's obvious that you've talked to someone, so you know she did." Jack squinted with a grimace.

"You're right, I heard that you two were together and that she double crossed you," Drake stated matter-of-fact, then continued, "But you tell me what happened. From your perspective."

"It doesn't really matter anymore," Jack pushed away again from the van, glancing to the side as he stepped away from Drake, "I got caught, I did my time. She got away with it. Simple as that."

"She stole money from you?"

"Yeah, she stole money from me-" Jack's face puffed up with anger, as he turned again to face him, "But it wasn't enough to just steal from me, she had the nerve to turn me in. And to him, no less."

"The agent?" Drake prompted.

"Yeah-" As he listened to the string of profanity that erupted from Jack at the mention of the other guy and his relationship with Natalie, Drake realized that, while he wouldn't allow himself to use the same words, he had to admit he had felt similar sentiments about Natalie and her relationship with Rolph Sartell.

Deception and betrayal were hard pills to swallow.

"But did you ever hear where she went after you were sent away? Did she end up with him?"

"I don't know. I heard he was married, but I think they were in it together - him turning a blind eye to her robbing me and then them getting together in the end. I think they had it all figured out to take me down. They probably split the money up between 'em."

"Did you have any evidence of that?"

"Well, no, not really. But there was plenty of talk from guys 'round here about it. It was just a little too coincidental, if you know what I mean. First, I figure out she's the one who ripped me off, next thing I know, I'm being busted."

"And after you were sent away, did she ever reach out to you or anyone else around here?"

"You kidding me? Hell, no. She was gone before I was even arrested. Never heard another word from her."

"Well," Drake glanced at the expansive rows of moving vans and rental equipment, "from the looks of it, you're better off without her."

"Yeah, that's an understatement," Jack Dawson squinted at Drake and asked, "You've asked lots of questions, now it's my turn. What happened with you and Natalie? Did she con you too?"

"No, I think she found a bigger fish and moved on before she figured out something that would work on me."

"Well, aren't you the lucky guy." His voice dripped with sarcasm as he drew on his cigarette.

"Yeah, I guess. Trouble was, she was my wife. I loved her."

"Yeah, she sure was easy to look at, but man, that broad was slippery. At first, I had a hard time with it all, I couldn't believe she did it. Eventually, I just started to hate her."

The words sent a shiver through Drake. Hatred was a fine line away from murder, given the proper encouragement. Not convinced yet that Jack Dawson was innocent in Natalie's crime, Drake pursued his line of questioning again.

"Jack, did you know she was back in Minnesota four years ago?"

"No, I was doing time."

Running out of patience, or maybe it was lack of interest, Jack Dawson crushed the cigarette butt in the gravel beneath his boot and dismissed Drake with his gaze.

"Look, I gotta get back to work. I don't know why you're here asking me all this about Natalie, but I was done with her a long time ago. As far as I'm concerned, good riddance."

He started to turn away and Drake stepped after him and instinctively reached for his elbow.

"Hey, Jack, one more thing-" With the sudden touch, Jack turned and glared at Drake's hand until he dropped it and held it up in careful retreat, as he asked, "What's the name of that agent she was with?"

"Now, you give me one good reason why I should tell you anything else." Jack Dawson uttered, his voice surly and callous.

Unprepared for his response, Drake shrugged.

"I don't have a good reason. Just curious, I guess." Drake offered honestly as he set his hands on his hips.

"Sheesh," Jack shook his head in disgust, "and I thought she messed me up bad." With that, he turned and walked towards the store.

Once he reached the back door, however, he paused and then called over his shoulder without looking back.

"Jeremy Hawthorne. Lives in Bloomington. Look him up."

The door slammed with a heavy thud behind him.

Chapter 17

2019

Sella & Drake

"I realize you didn't want to go into much detail with my brother, but I'm dying to know more about what happened with Jack Dawson." Sella prompted as soon as Drake's car door shut. Part of her hesitated to ask too many questions, wanting to respect his privacy, but a bigger part of her felt comfortable enough to expect he'd answer whatever she asked.

Drake pressed the ignition button and cranked the air conditioning, politely directing the vents her direction, to ward against the late morning humidity and simmering sunshine.

For a moment, he sat still in profile, his forehead furrowed and his eyes straight ahead, deep in thought. Her mind rolling through all kinds of scenarios of his visit, and stymied by his frozen silence, Sella's mind hesitated awkwardly on the realization that Drake Connor was an incredibly attractive man. He had the most impressive profile, a strong brow and distinct cheekbones above his trim mustache and beard.

When he turned to look at her, his light blue eyes were burning with the same intensity that she'd seen often with him and she had the vaguely intimidating feeling that nothing was out of reach for this man if he set his mind to it.

"Yes, I will tell you more about what happened," And then, as if he'd put his whole plan of next steps together within the span of these few seconds and found peace with it, Drake smiled a flash of white that brought heat to her face as if she was too close to a fire, "But first, do you know of any good places to eat around here? I'm starving."

They talked about many things that day. Over lunch, Drake relayed for her what sounded like a word for word summary of Jack Dawson's conversation. Then they discussed his plan to use his company's background-check service and social media search to find Jeremy Hawthorne and his plan to contact him.

As they drove the winding road through the forest towards Twin Shores, the topic of Natalie's disappearance pretty much exhausted, they talked about everything else.

Drake Connor, she decided, was a paradox. A mix of head-strong determination, and bold, almost youthful, indiscriminate courage, at the same time, he had a gentle vulnerability that spilled out in the most endearing ways, usually when he spoke about how important God was to him and how he tried to follow his will in the decisions he made each day.

He told her about his family – his parents Rita and Duncan, his sister Miranda, who farmed with his parents and her husband Caleb and their daughter Nina. They discussed his business Connor-Denning Security and how he had risked starting it many years ago after leaving a good paying job but never regretted it for a moment. Well, at least not until he had to make his first payroll, he said with a laugh.

Drake told her about how he met Natalie at a friend's block party in a west Chicago suburb - she lived next door – and that he'd fallen for her immediately and they were married six short months later, even though he freely admitted now that it was a blind attraction, not based on prayerful purpose.

When he talked about Natalie from this period of his life – as his wife and alive with unlimited potential for a happy life together - his mouth softened into a sad smile and his enthusiasm dimmed a little, like the battery behind the light of his eyes was weakened. It made Sella sad to see the effect it had on him.

They avoided discussion of their divorce, Natalie's disappearance, and the fact that he had been a prime suspect in it. He had already shared the broad outlines of that, and Sella wished to avoid causing him further pain by asking more probing questions about any of it.

About mid-way on their trip back to Twin Shores, they stopped to fill with gasoline and when they resumed the drive again, Drake turned the conversation towards her.

Talking about Henri and her family was always easy for her but talking about Garrett was never easy. Somehow that afternoon though, in the comfort of his car while staring out the passenger side window, Sella told him things that only people closest to her would know.

Maybe it helped that she shared a similar faith in God and that she felt secure he wouldn't judge her. It also helped that he had come out of a broken marriage with its own set of deception and lies. For whatever reason, she stepped out into the vast wilderness called vulnerability, encouraged by his embrace of it, and just started stringing thoughts and memories together as soon as they came to her mind.

Like how insecure she felt as a young woman and how Garrett made her feel special and cherished. How he'd travelled with his job as a broker with a national forfeiture firm, leaving her home alone with Henri for weeks at a time, but convinced her that he didn't have a choice and it was for their greater good financially.

She confessed to Drake that she had suspected infidelity over the years they were married but never had proof. Garrett always had an answer to everything, each suspicious restaurant and hotel receipt was explained away, flight itineraries to locations hours away from where he said he'd be were "last-minute meeting changes" and the "work" cell phone that he would never unlock was locked "for security reasons."

"So, were you surprised when he left, and he never came back?" Drake asked quietly, averting his eyes from hers to watch a car pass in front of them as they sat at a stop sign, not far from her house. If Sella wasn't mistaken, he was intentionally avoiding her gaze, giving her extra time to answer without having to look him in the eyes as she did so.

"Yes, I was surprised. Even after living with him for all those years, and all the excuses he made and the lies he told me, I still expected him to come back to us one day." Sella felt tears in the corner of her eyes brushing onto her eyelashes and was suddenly grateful he wasn't looking at her as she wiped them quickly away, "I *wanted* him to come back. Even after all that."

"Yeah, I get it. I really do." Drake eased the car onto the road that would finally end up at her driveway, "And I'm sure your family and friends have told you a million times, but allow this stranger-slash-new friend to add my two cents – you were too good for him, Gisella. Way too good for him. Not even in the same league, in my opinion."

Directing his brilliant blue eyes her way again, Drake smiled at her like she was his little sister and if they weren't in the car, he'd grab her around the shoulders into a big hug and ruffle her hair, while laughing that deep, full baritone laugh he had.

At least that's the feeling she got when he smiled at her that way. That look made her feel safe. It wasn't heavy or complicated and a small piece of her spirit lifted with that look and the easy friendship she felt with him.

But, at the same time, part of her sighed with a secret longing for a very different look in his eyes when he met her gaze. She realized that she missed it – someone looking at her *that* way.

***

Sitting at the small kitchen table the next day, Drake contemplated the tidy yard outside the paned window of his rental house. Perched on the edge of town at the end of a cul de sac with thick evergreens abutting the back yard, the house was a comfortable combination of northern Minnesota daily life and vacation life with its barbecue grill on the concrete patio and beach towels in the hall closet.

Frowning deeply in thought, he turned his attention to his laptop again and clicked through the pictures he found of Jeremy Hawthorne on Facebook. A forty-five-year old guy, with an average build and thick, dark hair peppered with gray, he seemed to be living the good life. At least that's what it looked like, judging by all the heart emojis his wife posted in her comments on his posts.

Here he was - this guy who supposedly had an affair with the subject of a drug investigation all those years ago -now living in the suburbs with a pretty wife, two cute kids and a dog... exactly what Drake had expected he and Natalie would be doing at this point in their lives.

Drake sighed and reached for his phone again as he read the background search email that listed Jeremy Hawthorne's current employment as simply "US Federal Agency" and included his address and telephone number.

It was seven-thirty in the morning. Not knowing if this number was for a cell phone or landline, Drake wondered, what were the chances he would be home? And, if so, what were the chances he would talk once Drake told him his reason for calling?

He reviewed his questions again in his mind - all he needed to do was find out if they had kept in touch after the affair. Just try to find out if it was possible Jeremy Hawthorne might be involved with Natalie's disappearance and accident. And if he smelled the hint of something like that, Drake would sic Detective Miller on him.

Besides, Jeremy Hawthorne seemed to be the only other person from Minnesota who had been connected to Natalie. So, if she wasn't travelling here to meet up with him, then she must have just taken this route on her way to the Canadian border.

But, if it was so simple, then why was he having such a hard time making this call?

Truth was, Drake was beginning to question his motivations for even coming to Minnesota in the first place. He set the phone down on the table as he pondered the Hawthorne family picture on Facebook again.

Last evening after he dropped Gisella off at her house, he had taken a left and gone deeper into the woods when he normally should have taken a right towards town. The scenic route took him on a winding path that knocked off his sense of direction, and he found himself completely lost in the trees.

He had eventually pulled his car off the gavel road into a rest area and sat on the rustic wooden bench that had been donated by the local fire department according to the metal plaque fastened to it. For a few minutes, he forced his mind to quiet down as he listened intently to the sounds of the wind playing amongst the leaves of the birch and the rustle of the towering pines. It reminded him of times as a kid when he would listen to the crackling rustle of harvest-ready corn leaves swishing against each other in the autumn breeze.

As he contemplated where he stood with this quest, Drake found himself begging God for some degree of peace about all of this. He kept asking himself the disconcerting question, was it right for him to be so obsessive about their failed marriage and Natalie's eventual death? What was it doing to his walk with God and to his relationships with others that he could not seem to let it go? Wasn't it self-serving - and a sin - to wallow in this wounded pride and anger?

And, as he considered what Gisella had shared about her lying cheat of a husband and her own failed marriage, it forced him to put his own marriage in clearer focus and the analysis was straightforward.

Question: What were his feelings for Natalie and his memories of their relationship based on anyway?

Answer: Lies and half-truths.

If he had ever gotten to know the *real* Natalie - the Natalie these people from her past had known so very well - would he have fallen in love with her in the first place? And, most importantly, would he have asked her to be his wife?

Drake picked up his phone again. He would try to tread lightly with Jeremy Hawthorne, but he had to make this one last attempt before he gave up and returned home.

It took two rings before the sound of a Bluetooth car speaker picked up the call, obviously, this was his cell phone number.

"Hello, Hawthorne here."

"Hello, Agent Hawthorne. This is Drake Connor. You don't know me, but we have both known someone who's recently passed away and I wanted to ask you a few questions."

"Okay... what did you say your name is?"

"Drake Connor. Many years ago, you knew my ex-wife Natalie."

Shocked silence.

But his silence didn't surprise Drake; in fact, it energized him as he continued boldly, "Natalie went missing a few years ago and was found in a submerged car in northern Minnesota this past spring. You probably know all about that though. I think it made the local news."

"Okay," Hawthorne hedged cautiously, "I don't know how you got my number, but if this person was involved in a previous case I worked, you know I can't talk about it."

"No, I completely understand," Drake forced an agreeable tone into his voice, "you don't have to tell me about the case. I've already talked to the subject of your investigation, Jack Dawson."

"Well – again, I won't talk about my cases so I would appreciate if you don't call me–"

"I don't care about the case, Agent," Drake interrupted smoothly, "Jack Dawson already told me all about the investigation that sent him to jail. And I'm guessing, he deserved it. But that's not important to me. I'm calling you to ask if you kept in touch with Natalie after Jack went to prison."

"I – well, I don't know who you're talking about. I don't remember a person name Natalie–" Jeremy Hawthorne faltered, leaning heavily into the act of denial.

"See, I don't believe that," Drake interrupted again, even more confidently, "I think you *do* remember her. She's hard to forget. Jack seemed to think Natalie was your informant and that you went over easy on her for some reason. He theorized that she was *more* than just an informant. But again, I don't care what happened between you two during that investigation. I'm just wondering if she might have been back in Minnesota four years ago to see you."

Long silence.

This time Drake allowed himself a glimmer of hope that Jeremy might make a mistake. He just might let something slip.

"Look, I don't have to tell you anything, Mr. Connor-"

"You're right, you don't. Your cooperation would just help us answer some questions about the last months of her life. She's gone now anyway so whatever relationship you had with her years ago is water under the bridge-"

"Yes, that's right," Jeremy interrupted brashly, "It was many years ago, and the investigation was closed without incident. That's all I'm going to say."

"But was it 'without incident,' as you say?" Drake pressured, feeling like he might be on to something, "You see, Natalie and I met in Chicago years after this drug bust and she never mentioned any of it to me. That makes me wonder if the investigation was all kosher – like, maybe something wasn't handled properly."

"I don't know what you mean by that and I don't want to encourage this conversation any further-"

"See, the detectives are looking into Natalie's death and the people she knew," This was a bluff, so Drake cautioned himself not to push too hard before continuing, "It's made me wonder, was Natalie blackmailing you, Agent Hawthorne?"

"What?" Jeremy Hawthorne growled the word with disgust.

"Was she blackmailing you about the affair you two had and the money that was rumored to go missing during the drug bust?"

"I don't know what you're talking-"

"Because I think after they speak to Jack Dawson, that's what they will ask you."

"I didn't steal- I don't know what you're talking about-"

"But, like I said, I don't care about that drug bust. I'm just wondering if you talked to her four years ago when she came back to Minnesota?"

"No! The answer to that question is emphatically, No. Now, really, Mr. Connor, or whoever you are, lose my number. Don't call me again."

The phone line went dead, and Drake swiped the call closed on his cell phone as he breathed a deep sigh, slightly shaken by intensity of emotion.

Well, that's it then, his mind quelled his roaring spirit. His quest was finished, and he didn't have any more answers than when he arrived a few weeks ago.

Did he believe that Agent Hawthorne - suburban dad and upstanding law enforcement official with the beautiful family, who were most likely clueless about his past – did he believe that he was telling him the truth?

No.

Was there anything he could do about it?

Not really.

CHAPTER 18

2011 – mid 2013

Natalie

So, the time in Minnesota got a little crazy when Jack was sent to prison. I learned that dealing illegal drugs is a rough business with some really rough people, but I came out of it with more cash than I'd ever had.

TC and I had begun to fall into old habits by then. He lived in Minnesota too, under a different name and cover, and we were basically together again. It was almost transactional to him. I didn't want to contemplate what it was doing to me.

One morning, I overheard him on the phone, and I knew he was talking to another woman. He even told her that he loved her.

I told myself I didn't care.

So, I bolted. Things were way too hot in Minnesota anyway.

I moved to Chicago and met the owner of an entertainment company that put on shows for big-ticket rock bands. I had my degree and the chit chat that went along with it, so I got a job in his accounting department before the end of our second date.

The guy was a real piece of work. One of the meanest men I'd ever done business with. Which made stealing his money that much sweeter.

There were a couple more marks in and around Chicago, but by 2011, I was getting tired.

I went through a self-administered self-analysis and eventually I decided that my weariness with this "life" must be an indication that I needed a change.

But it wasn't just a change of address or a change of job that I needed. I decided what I needed was a complete make-over - I needed to change who I was. Instead of looking for a mark when I went out, I went out looking for a husband.

It didn't happen right away. It took much longer than I expected – certainly much longer than finding a mark.

But when I met Drake that day at my neighbor's house, I knew he was the one.

Even though my initial motivation to marry him was more righteous than to steal from him, I must admit I was tempted to mark him after I found out that he owned a company with his business partner and was relatively wealthy.

Often, I saw opportunities to scam him because he was so trusting. From the very beginning, he acted like so many of the others; he just couldn't see me. It was like he refused to see the real me.

The trouble with Drake, and the reason I couldn't mark him, was that he broke the golden rule.

He wasn't dirty.

A few months later, we were married, and I was miserable.

Every day I was miserable. And when I say that I mean I was so depressed, I often thought about suicide.

Anything, just so I wouldn't have to look at the man who was my husband.

I tried to be the person he was imagining when he looked at me. I tried to resist the desire to scratch his kind eyes out of their sockets. I'd leave the room, I'd leave the house, I'd leave the city. Anything to be away from the reflection of myself that I saw in his eyes.

He loved me and I hated him for it.

I'd lie in bed next to him, listening to him sleeping and all I could think about was that night when I was fourteen years old and I killed a man. And how I enjoyed it. How, if I had the chance, I would do it all over again. And again, and again.

It didn't matter that I was married to Drake, I was still seeing TC when the opportunity presented itself, just to keep my sanity. Besides, TC always knew when I needed him — he had the uncanny way of knowing when I was crawling out of my skin in suburbia.

When he called me around my first anniversary, he told me he had a job for us. I told him maybe I should stay clean because I was married, and that Drake was a good guy. He said he didn't want to hear about Drake, and he could care less that I was married.

He told me marriage was just a piece of paper and he assured me that he could change my name and make it like the marriage never even happened. That's how inconsequential my marriage was to him.

He said he had a "special" mark for me, and it would take some effort and patience to set the hook. This mark was man in Chicago, and he was a big one.

His name was Rolph Sartell.

CHAPTER 19

2019

Sella

"Dad, please get out of bed, it's almost nine o'clock. We gotta get moving, they expected me at the office over an hour ago!"

Sella rapped her knuckles on her father's bedroom door and listened for a response, or some sign to assure her that he was getting dressed. When she heard nothing, she abruptly pushed open the door with an impatient sigh.

Seeing the rounded shape of his form under his blankets, she moved quickly across the room towards his bed and placed her hand on his slim shoulder as she tried to rustle him awake. After a moment, Luca moaned and squeezed his closed eyes tighter together with a frown, ignoring her like she was a pesky fly.

"Dad, you haven't moved an inch since I was in here half an hour ago! Come on, Dad," She entreated as she sat on the edge of his bed and patted his shoulder firmly again, "I need you to get up now."

"I can't, Sella. I'm just too tired – let me sleep a little longer."

"But you've been sleeping since seven o'clock last night. You can't be that tired!"

"But I am tired, you just go without me, I will stay home with your mother–" Luca murmured, turned his mouth into a lazy grin, and buried his head further in his pillow as he disappeared into a sleep-hazed memory.

"Dad, you know I can't leave you home-" Sella's voice dropped off as she listened to him snoring softly and conceded to herself that she wasn't going to make it to the office today. Again. This was the fourth time in the past two weeks that she was unable to get him out of bed in the morning.

He was getting worse. The lack of energy and appetite had come on strong this summer. Things he used to do just a few months ago - like mowing the lawn or going fishing at the river with Henri – now seemed like a steep climb to him. If she would encourage him to do some of the activities he used to love doing, he would look at her with a blank stare and sometimes his response would be a pitifully weak smile. It was almost as if he was trying to be courteous listener, but he couldn't understand the foreign language she was speaking.

"Okay, Dad," Sella patted his shoulder before leaning in to kiss his warm forehead, "You just sleep for a little while longer. I'll tell them that we might get to the shop later this afternoon."

Sella crossed the room and with a last glance at her father's sleeping figure, she pulled the door closed behind her.

Continuing to the kitchen, Sella glanced out the window to find Henri waiting patiently on the tire swing that hung on the big elm tree that shaded the garage.

He's going to miss softball practice again today, Sella noted sadly. She was planning to drop him off at the park on her way to the shop this morning and now that wouldn't happen either.

As she pulled her lap top out of her work bag and plugged it into the wall outlet next to her dining room table, Sella rapped on the window and motioned for him to come back inside.

He wouldn't be too happy, but Henri was used to sacrificing things for his Poppy. She'd have to make it up to him somehow, like go for a picnic at the river later this afternoon.

When he joined her in the kitchen, Sella said, "Sorry, bud, Poppy's not able to get out of bed this morning so we won't get into town for practice. I will text your coach, ok? I'm sure he will understand."

"Again?" Henri asked and then tried to overcome his disappointment as he sighed dramatically, "He sure is sleeping a lot."

"I know. I think it's the new pills they have him on for his memory," Sella reached out towards him and ruffled through his thick, dark hair, "I will make sure that we get you to practice tomorrow though, okay? I know you can't miss practices if you want to play Saturday."

"Yeah, that's what coach says. I think I will get to play short stop. That's an important position, mom."

"It sure is," Sella bent down and kissed the top of his head before shifting away and looking him directly in the eyes, "Thanks, Henri."

"For what?" Henri asked, his eyebrows furrowed in confusion, "What did I do?"

"You're just are a good kid, that's all. You give up stuff because of Poppy, you know he can't help it, and you just understand things. You're a good kid, Henri. I love you." Sella drew him closer to her and hugged him tightly.

"Okay, well, whatever, Mom," He allowed her to hug him but then pulled away with a grin and excitement bubbling in his voice, "Guess what I saw this morning?"

"No clue." Sella turned her attention to the computer screen that was coming to life on the table behind her.

"I saw some new tracks in that mud behind the birch trees. I think it might be a moose. I want to track him."

"Oh, really? Well, be careful, Henri. You know the rules, take your phone and I will call for you in an hour. I expect you to answer, okay?"

"No problem. Thanks, Mom." He called over his shoulder, but his voice was muted because he was already out the door.

As she watched him shoot across the back yard on his way towards the birch grove, Sella thought again about the conversation she had with Drake the other day during their drive from Hibbing.

It wasn't easy working full-time, raising Henri and taking care of her father. Sometimes she felt like a machine, programmed to get up each day and do the tasks required of her until it was time to go to bed where she would regenerate and start all over again the next morning. Honestly, she wasn't complaining about her life because she whole-heartedly recognized that God had blessed her with so much.

No, it wasn't a complaint she had for God, it was more of a question that she had been contemplating recently.

Yesterday, when she caught her reflection in the mirror, she stopped and really looked at herself. Her blonde bangs were getting a little long and as she smoothed them to the side of her face, she smiled at the reflection and realized that for the first time in many years, she actually liked the person she saw reflected in the mirror.

Was there something else for her in this life, another level of connection to someone else that she had been missing since Garrett left? Were these questions the beginning of a renewal, a deeper relationship with God and the realization that she could meet someone else to share life with?

It felt scary to her, no doubt. In fact, she felt decidedly nauseous at the very concept. But maybe that nauseous feeling was simply nerves? A good kind of nerves. Like the cliché' butterflies that seemed the best description anyone had come up with to describe the sensation.

"I *could* fall in love again." Sella whispered aloud to the silent house.

She put her fingers to her lips as if to swallow the words back up again but when she touched them, she found her lips were locked into a smile.

Yes. If the right man came along, she was reasonably sure she could fall in love again.

At least she was starting to think it a possibility and that was a complete reversal of where she'd been just a few weeks ago, she thought as she focused on her computer again.

She didn't stop to contemplate what the past few weeks meant or why her perspective on pursuing a relationship was softening. But the words that Drake had casually dropped into their conversation the other day were somehow responsible, and they continued to play around in her memory as she reviewed her email.

You were too good for him, Gisella, way too good for him.

Those words from a relative stranger – a very attractive male stranger - made her feel appreciated and special and it was almost embarrassingly simple. It seemed that hearing those words was all it took to soften her resolve and open her mind to the possibility of finding someone again.

***

"Surprise!" The guests shouted as Coop and his wife Val walked through the vine-rimmed archway of the restaurant's outdoor patio. As the initial shock wore off, Coop glanced at his wife with a broad smile.

"You got me! I don't know how you did it, but you got me!"

Val had sent email invitations to thirty of Coop's closest friends and family so the patio was packed with guests, all friends, family and co-workers from the sheriff's department. After making her way through the crowd and greeting various people she knew, Sella found a seat across the long table from her brother Phillip.

"Where's Pat tonight?" Sella asked him, as she reached for a menu that was propped between bottles of ketchup and barbecue sauce.

"She's working night shifts this month," He replied as he set his readers on his nose and appraised the menu. After twenty years, he was quite used to the crazy work schedule of his wife, the nurse.

"Oh, that's right," Sella remembered her telling her that the other day when she stopped at the shop before heading to the hospital, "I was talking to Pat the other day about Dad's patterns changing and she said I should make another appointment with his doctor to review the meds."

"Again? Didn't you just bring him in last month?"

"Yes, but something isn't quite right. You know how he is sleeping all the time? And this weekend, he didn't even want to go to Duluth for his week at Reese's house. He's always been excited to go before."

"Yeah, I know, I've noticed some changes too. In fact, Sella, we've been talking - Sebastian, Reese and I. We think it's time to think about moving Dad to a place that can help him 24/7. Not that you aren't helping him, but you know-"

Phillip left his comment open-ended with a sad lift of one shoulder and shook his head slightly.

So, they'd been talking, huh? Sella couldn't help feeling hurt that they'd felt the need to have this conversation without her. It didn't really surprise her that they were at this point, she had been expecting the day to come when they would all decide it was time to move their father to a care center, but she just wasn't prepared for it to come so quickly.

"Yeah, we should talk," Sella conceded grudgingly, "Maybe on Labor Day weekend. You still want everyone to come to your cabin?"

"Yeah, that's the plan-" Phillip replied.

"So, thanks for coming, guys!" Coop interrupted as he sat down next to Sella at the table, not realizing they were in the middle of a serious conversation.

"Well, happy birthday, Coop," Sella said, not upset at the interruption, she would have plenty of time to discuss this with Phillip and her other brothers. As she took a quick drink of water, she smiled up at Coop, "Were you really surprised, or was that an act you put on a few minutes ago?"

"No, that was no act! She totally surprised me with this one. Besides, you know very well that I can't act. Nothing like your eldest brother here; he was the lead in the senior play. I did the stage lights, remember?"

Phillip's face flushed at the memory and he rolled his eyes with a laugh.

"Oh, yes," Sella goaded, "the memory of that play is emblazoned forever on the minds of the audience. The stage hasn't seen the likes of that talent since."

As the two old friends took a quick detour down memory lane, Sella caught sight of Coop's wife Val a few feet away and walking alongside her a man, her hand on his elbow, directing him toward their table.

He was nice looking with light-colored hair, slim and tall, dressed in neat, dark jeans and a crisp white dress shirt. It was the look on Val's face as she caught Sella's attention that gave it away. Sella was sure of what was coming before a word was said.

"Oh, well, look who's here," Coop gave Sella a side glance, crinkled his eye into a wink and stood to greet the two, "Glad you could make it Zachary. Here, let me introduce you. You know Phillip, of course. And, this is his sister, Sella. I don't think you've met her yet. Sella, this is Deputy Zachary Wyler. He's new in town, from Duluth."

Zachary Wyler stretched out his hand and smiled rather sheepishly. Obviously, this was a set-up and both Sella and Zachary Wyler knew it.

But Zachary didn't seem to mind, judging by the bright smile that stayed fixed on his mouth. He seemed so young, Sella thought to herself, could he even be thirty years old? He had a nice smile though, she conceded grudgingly in her mind, and lively green eyes too.

"Nice to meet you, Sella." He shook her hand formally and then shifted aside as the waitress passed to take the orders of people seated at the table behind them.

"Same, nice to meet you too." Sella smiled back at him as she feigned ignorance of the motivation behind Val bringing him over to greet them.

"Are you here solo tonight, Zachary?" Phillip spoke up from his place across the table. Feeling cornered by her brother and his friend the birthday boy, Sella narrowed her eyes into a frown. Phillip knew full well Zachary was here alone tonight, but he acted surprised and pleased by his affirmative nod. "Really? Well, why don't you join us? They're taking food orders now." He gestured to the open chair next to Sella.

"Sure. That is if you don't mind, Sella?" Zachary's question as he glanced at the empty chair was obviously meant to be polite but came off a bit awkward as he fumbled with the chair that had become lodged on the leg of the table.

"No, of course not, go ahead," Sella said and turned in her seat to face her brother with a look of frustration at this whole situation.

What was she going to do about it though? Rather than make this all awkward, she reasoned she might as well just play along with their little game. Given her earlier resolution to put herself "out there" again, she figured this was as good a place to start as any.

And she was surprised to admit after the party began to wind down a while later, it wasn't all that bad. She might even say that it was rather enjoyable.

Zachary was easy to look at, easy to talk to and easy to like. She found out that her first impression was right – he was younger than her by three years, he'd never been married and had no children. He said that, although he worked a lot, he was looking forward to exploring more of the woods and fishing on the lakes in the area and he especially loved to canoe and camp.

In fact, they got along so well, it wasn't even surprising to her that Zachary asked her for her number and floated the idea of them getting together for a hike or canoe ride later in the week.

What surprised Sella was how excited she felt at the prospect of a first date. And she owed it all to Drake.

Chapter 20

2019

Sella & Drake

It was time to go home, Drake thought as he sent an email response to his Minneapolis team at the close of business that Friday.

In his mind, he worked through his upcoming schedule. They had issues with some new software at the office in Minneapolis that he would work through before heading back to the Chicago office where they were dealing with a few more fires. Although he was mentally beating himself up about being absent from work when they needed him, Drake didn't feel guilty. Even though his quest in Minnesota hadn't clarified anything regarding Natalie's reasons for being here before she died, his time here had been exactly what he needed.

Not that he'd call it closure. It was more like a puzzle that was coming together slowly. Drake was sure it would never be complete and fully visible, but every person he'd talked to offered him more pieces of Natalie that helped him organize her life into something that made more sense.

Why she lived like this before she knew him and why, suddenly one day, she picked up that life again with Rolph Sartell he would never understand. *The difficult thing was, he would just have to accept that he would never understand.*

Over the past two days, he'd spent time hiking and meditating on stories of sorrow from the Bible, including Job and Joseph. As he read the Bible scriptures, the lessons of their lives landed heavy on his spirit. They hadn't given in to the temptation of worldly sorrow as Paul described in 2 Corinthians, where one focuses on oneself. Instead, the stories of Job and Joseph showed men who practiced Godly sorrow. Though they suffered immensely, they had not focused on themselves but instead had turned more fully to God, begging forgiveness, and finding God's comfort.

That was the way he wanted to live. Moving past the past and on towards the future.

More than once, he had picked up his phone intending to call Gisella - just wanting to hear her voice, maybe to ask if she'd join him for a hike - but each time, he stopped short of dialing her number. Something about drawing her further into this very personal part of his life felt wrong. He told himself that he was leaving soon, and since there was such a physical distance between Chicago and Twin Shores, it was probably best to put an emotional distance between the two of them as well.

But even as the thought filtered through his mind again, he found himself dialing her number.

Just one last visit to say goodbye, he told himself. *That was to be expected and only cordial, right?* He would miss Henri and Luca. And her. He would especially miss her.

Drake found himself holding his breath during the long moments it took for her phone to ring.

"Hello, Drake." She answered, her mellow voice laced with a hesitation that confirmed his mistake. He knew he should have reached out to her sooner in the week. Now, he'd offended her.

"Hey, Gisella. I've been meaning to call you."

"Yes, well, no problem, I know you're busy. How did your call with the DEA agent go?"

"It went nowhere actually." He admitted, trying not to sound defeated.

"Oh, sorry to hear that." She replied with an empathetic tone in her reserved voice.

"Yeah, well, that's the way it works out sometimes. I had hoped he might admit to something that would shed some light on it all, but he denied everything."

"Do you think he was lying to you?"

"Probably." *Not probably*, Drake was sure he was lying to him.

"Oh, that's too bad," Gisella paused, allowing Drake time to picture the concerned look in her deep brown eyes, before she continued, "I guess you will never know for sure, but at least you tried. Now that you've turned over the last stone, how do you feel?"

"Well, it's not easy, that's for sure," Drake confessed, unable to hold back his thoughts, "I have a lot of emotions about all of this stuff about Natalie. I've been confused, sad, angry – just so many emotions, you know?"

"Well, you're bound to have a lot of emotions, Drake. You've been bombarded with a ton of stuff you didn't know about your ex-wife," Gisella worked through the logic calmly, "But now that you know it, I hope you can see that it doesn't change who you are. It's who Natalie was and now she is gone."

"I know. You're right." Drake listened to his own response and frowned to himself - Did he sound hesitant? Even after learning all this about who Natalie was, could he possibly be holding onto the dream of what they had, the ghost that was never there?

"It's really not my place to offer advice, I know," Gisella's voice was quiet, yet firm, "but Drake, I think it's best for you to let this go."

"Yeah, you're right. I think I'm close to that now. Really."

"Good. I'm glad to hear you say it. She's gone, Drake. You deserve to live your life again. Without Natalie shadowing it."

"You know, it's strange. For the first time since she disappeared, I think I can actually see that happening. Living my life again, I mean."

As he said the words, pictures of a future played around the corners of his consciousness. The pause lengthened as he struggled to find words to fill his unease at the questions those pictures brought to his mind. He didn't see how this could work, but instinctively he knew he didn't want Gisella out of his life.

"So," Drake began, "I was wondering, are you busy this evening?"

Wow, that was smooth, he fumed to himself and rolled his eyes.

"Umm, yes, I am actually. Sorry." Sella seemed to falter in her response and Drake couldn't tell if it was because she was embarrassed by what sounded like a request for a date. His face flushed and he was glad that he wasn't standing in front of her so that she could witness his disappointment and humiliation.

"Oh, okay-"

"It's just – well, I have a date tonight-" She continued, her voice low and quiet, with the sound of a smile in it.

"Oh, really?" His heart plummeted for an unknown reason, but he did his best to recover by adding with a rueful laugh, "Anyone I know?"

"Ha, ha, as if you know anyone around here," She joined in the joke, "Of course, you *may* have met him, he's a lawman."

"Seems like we've had this conversation before. I hope it's not that sheriff friend of yours. I thought you told me he was married."

"No, of course not! It's Coop's deputy." She laughed; the sound was disheartening, and a series of sharp regrets poisoned his mood. Unable to withstand the power of them, he named the regrets in his mind – one, it was another guy, not him that was taking her on a date. And two, he had to leave her here in Minnesota while he went home again.

"Oh, okay," Drake finally spoke, trying his best not to show his disappointment, "Well, in that case, I'll just say goodbye to you over the phone."

"What - you're leaving?"

"Yes, had to happen sometime, I guess."

"Yeah, I guess." Sella hesitated briefly, not saying any of the words that Drake would have wanted her to say, "When?"

"I guess I'm heading back to Minneapolis tomorrow to work out some things at the office there."

"Oh, okay. Well, I'm glad we met you, Drake."

"Me too," Drake paused, maybe he should say something about wanting her in his future somehow? Was that what he wanted? Even if it was what he wanted, it didn't seem like it was what she wanted.

So, he held his tongue, even though it was almost painful, "Say goodbye to Henri and Luca for me."

"I will do that."

"Tell them that if I'm ever in the neighborhood again, we need to go fishing so I can show them how to catch walleye."

"Okay-" She laughed, and the sound of it brought a flush to his face again and he noticed he missed seeing her face already.

"And Gisella?" Drake loved the way her name rolled on his tongue. Just saying it made him smile inside, despite his disappointment at this goodbye.

"Yes?" She sounded like she was smiling back at him.

"I hope you have fun on your date tonight. And just so you know, this lawman is a lucky guy."

"Well – thank you, Drake. Take care of yourself." Her words were carefully phrased with restraint.

"I will. Goodbye, Gisella."

Chapter 21

2014

Natalie

Rolph Sartell was a big name in the construction business. As Rolph liked to describe it, his company "moved ground around" for the some of the largest business developments in the country.

TC met Rolph while they were waiting for their flight in the executive lounge at an airport somewhere in Virginia. After a few rounds of drinks, it became obvious to TC that Rolph tended to drink too much and talk too much. Usually, these characteristics didn't get Rolph into trouble, but he had never met anyone like TC before.

As the flight landed in Chicago later that evening, TC had convinced Rolph that "his guy" could help Rolph make some serious side money in some investments (aka TC's ponzi scheme) and that they should meet again to discuss in more detail.

The line had been cast and the fish was sniffing the hook.

As he worked the mark, TC began to see a bit of dirt in Rolph Sartell, making him a prime target, and that's when he called me. He said he knew I was the perfect partner for this one, but Rolph must never know about our connection to one another.

I know I sound weak by saying this, but it felt good to be needed by TC. Even if it was just as an actor in the scam. So, I agreed.

Rolph, who had been divorced for a few years, was the "marrying kind" and couldn't resist a pretty face, according to TC. The first step for me would be to get a job at Rolph's company, then gain his trust and then get a ring. As in a wedding ring.

TC had full confidence in my ability to lure Rolph to fall in love with me and eventually fall into my trap. The fact that I was already married was of no consequence to him since I had already confessed that I didn't want to be married to Drake anyway.

It's no surprise you want to dump him, he said. You aren't wired to be a wife.

It was TC's idea to tell Rolph that my husband was abusive and that I felt unsafe in my marriage. TC was sure that Rolph would fall for the story because most men were suckers for feeling like they had to "save the damsel in distress."

I said to TC, why don't you ever feel like that?

He said, I'm not like most men. And you're nothing like other women.

I knew what he meant, and it wasn't a compliment about my looks.

Even though I knew he was right - that I had no heart - I did feel bad about using Drake like that. It was like kicking a puppy that trusted you. I've never been keen on animals of any kind, but I have to admit puppies can be cute sometimes.

The trouble with puppies, like husbands, is that they are needy. They expect things, they become dependent. I hate that about puppies. And husbands.

I started working for Rolph in 2013, after TC conveniently suggested to Rolph that he should use the same employment recruiter that I was listed *with. A few extra dollars thrown the way of the recruiter, and I was a shoo-in for the job.*

Once inside, I found that TC was right: Rolph was dirty and billed a lot of work off the books and was paid in cash. Some of the jobs were small, others were very large.

To gain Rolph's trust, at first, I just did my job. I took care of things for him and never asked questions. Soon, he was looking at me the way I wanted him to, spending time hanging around my desk at the office, bringing me cups of coffee. Within a few months, and a few stories of my horrible home life married to an ogre of a husband, we were having an affair, and everything was going according to plan.

By early 2014, I had done all I could to break Drake's heart -I told him I loved Rolph and had never loved him - and he finally gave me a divorce.

I know I make it sound easy, and mostly it was. There were only a few moments that it hurt. If I didn't have to look Drake in the eyes, I mostly forgot about those moments.

My work with Rolph was what was important, not Drake. I approached the job as I would anything else in my life of crime. I was intentional, strategic, and patient. My goal was to make him fall in love with me and I wanted to reach this goal in the worst way. It was a challenge for me - like some people challenge themselves to master golf or fly fishing.

The grooming process was not only challenging, it was also exciting. First, I had to insulate myself and Rolph from others in the office so that I was his primary confidant, and I became the communicator of all things financial. Then, I quietly started the inflated invoicing scam and siphoned off a steady stream of cash to my accounts. At the same time, I started to encourage more off-the-books work and watched as the off-the-books cash coffers grew.

Eventually my patience paid off. The day I knew Rolph trusted me was the day he gave me the passcodes for his safes. That was a good day and I celebrated with a massage and pedicure at the most exclusive spa I could find.

I laid there as the massage therapist kneaded the knots out of my neck and thought, Now I had the passcodes to his money and the keys to his heart.

"You done good, sweetie" as my southern mother would often say.

Rolph proposed to me in July 2015 while we spent the weekend at his place on Lake Tahoe. Over a candlelight dinner on the terrace with the mountains in the background, he told me that he loved me, and I told him "I love you too, sugar."

What else could I say? The diamond in that ring was enormous. I sure loved him for putting that on my finger.

CHAPTER 22

2015

Natalie

Since I encouraged a pre-nuptial agreement (an important step in the grooming process), I was completely trustworthy in Rolph's eyes. What he didn't know was that a pre-nup couldn't stop me from stealing from him right from under his nose.

With the money that I had embezzled and the jewelry Rolph had given me, along with the money in his personal and business safes, our total haul would be close to 1.2 million dollars. Rolph promised to be the biggest single mark I'd ever done by a long shot. The job was even more intoxicating because I was doing it alongside my boyfriend-partner.

TC was never just a crime partner to me. He was always my significant other, and not in the typical romantic way. Instead, it was clear to me that he held a part of me that no one else could ever dream to hold. And while he often handled me carelessly, he was unwilling to let me go. He wasn't shy about exerting his control over me and told me that it was for the good of both of us that I listen to him.

For example, I had married Drake without his knowledge; it wasn't part of his plan and he had always resented it. Look where that got you, he'd say with a casual shrug and a look of disdain.

With Rolph, it was different. In TC's mind, our marriage was never permanent. It was just part of the plan.

In fact, the morning of our wedding a few months later, TC surprised me by a visit to the house − thankfully, Rolph wasn't at home at the time. And even though Rolph now considered TC a friend, we had been very careful to never let Rolph know that we knew each other.

The day of my wedding, TC told me that he had a plan for how the whole thing would go down. He said once I stole the money that I should make my way to Sault Ste. Marie, then cross into Canada and head north and west. Then, we would meet up in Vancouver, Canada and he would make a way for us to disappear for good.

I was standing there in my robe, with rollers in my hair and the makeup artist I'd hired waiting for me upstairs in my bedroom. I couldn't believe what I was hearing.

"You mean you want us to go away together?"

"Yes."

"Like − as a couple? And - live together again?"

"Yes," He said, a smile lifting the corners of his mouth, "You act surprised."

"Shocked - is the word."

"Is that a yes?" He reached for me and pulled out a roller from my hair, running his fingers through the loose curl.

"You bet it's a yes, sugar."

I readily agreed because TC and I were the same and I knew he'd never let me go anyway. I knew my life was intertwined with his and that would never change.

I thought about it later - why would he choose to tell me the plan for the escape and his desire for us to be together on the day I was getting married to another man? I came to see it was the control he needed. Gradually, something about that recognition pinched me deep inside, and it felt strangely familiar and hurtful, but I let it go.

By then, I had convinced myself that I wasn't ever going to care about a man in a healthy, fulfilling way - where you built a life with someone based equal parts trust, respect and love – that kind of love was for other women, the ones without dirty secrets.

I knew what I meant to him. It was business; a sick, twisted business where we were bound together, unable to extricate ourselves from each other.

Of course, that day and every day after that day, I knew I wasn't the only woman in his life, but I didn't ask him about the woman who heard the words, "I love you too."

I didn't know if he held something over her like he did me, but I guessed he must because I couldn't see TC being with someone unless he could control her like that.

The longer I thought about it, the less I wanted to know anything about her. So, eventually, I didn't think about her at all.

CHAPTER 23

Fall 2019

Drake

It was a remarkably lazy Saturday morning in late October. The sunshine rippled through the blinds, their dance across the polished concrete floor ending at the couch where he sat, feet up on the ottoman. In fact, it was the first Saturday in the past two months that he had allowed himself to chill at home instead of heading into the office and it felt good.

Reaching for his coffee cup on the sofa table to the right of his shoulder, Drake glanced up from the Chicago Tribune website on his tablet to check out the notification beep from his personal email account. With a smile, he opened the email from Henri, which was sent using his mother's email account because she didn't allow her son to use any other electronic means of communication.

It was another email about fishing, another in a string of many videos that were forwarded to him over the past few months since he left Minnesota. This time the link took Drake to an ice fishing video filmed on some backcountry lake somewhere in northern Russia. Not a word of English was spoken in the video, but that didn't seem to matter to Henri. He said what was interesting was the way they dug their holes in the ice, using a lightweight auger that attached to a hand drill. He wondered in his adorably stilted email if Drake had ever used something like that when he went ice fishing?

As he typed his reply, - No, he hadn't used that type of tool to open a hole in the ice, but it sure looked easier than dragging around a heavy ice auger - Drake wondered again about the woman whose email account was being used by her 10-year old son.

He wondered if she read the email correspondence between Henri and him and if she was ever tempted to write one of her own. Because he was sorely tempted to write to her.

They had texted a few times, at first it was to exchange email addresses and then it was "to catch up." But that's all that came of it. They had both moved on from the friendship (that's all it could be called, right?) that had developed during his summer quest.

Gisella was dating the deputy, a guy named Zachary, and she seemed content and happy.

Drake on the other hand, was working too much to consider dating and was in a state of what he called semi-happy, but definitely not content. At least not in the relationship department.

The problem was clear. Even though his calendar – his life - was wide open, ready to meet someone, his heart was not.

And, if he was honest, for years his heart had been bound up in unresolved feelings for Natalie, now it was stymied by undefined feelings for Gisella.

Of course, whenever this recognition resurfaced - like when he read an email from her adorable son - he worked hard to shut the indecision down again - bury the feelings deep - and go back to work.

Sighing, Drake pushed the ottoman away with his stockinged feet and reached for his shoes.

It would be a good time to go the office, no one would be there on Saturday morning.

He had things to do and people to forget.

CHAPTER 24

2015

Natalie

December 15, 2015. That's the day we chose.

Rolph was scheduled to be away on a week-long business trip to New Orleans, leaving me, his trusted accountant and doting wife, all alone at the office.

For the past year, TC and I had been using burner phones to communicate so there would be no record of our relationship to one another and we hadn't even seen one another in person since the day of the wedding months before.

We discussed that I would pack my car to look like I was headed on a ski trip and hide the money in a cooler in the back hatch of my car. I would cross the US - Canadian border using a false passport he sent me and once over the border, I'd ditch my car for a different one using a car dealership that he had "prearranged." Using the other false passport and a driver's license he had given me, I was supposed to make my way west through Canada towards Vancouver where I would wait at a house he'd already rented under a false identity. That's where he'd meet me.

January 20, 2016. That was the date we were supposed to meet up at his house in Vancouver.

That was the day we would begin our life together. Again.

Just like in Charlotte.

CHAPTER 25

November 2019

Drake

"Myles, you guys just get started, I'll join you in a few minutes. I have to return a few calls first." Drake gathered the used food containers and napkins into a garbage can before sitting back down at his desk. They had just finished lunch from the new Chinese place down the street. And although their egg rolls left something to be desired, they sure made a killer sesame chicken, Drake thought as he moved aside some papers to reach for his message slips.

He looked over the messages that his receptionist Rene had taken during their lunch meeting. After a few calls to customers and one to his church to inquire about an upcoming Bible study his men's group was having, Drake stood, gathered his computer tablet, and dropped his cell phone in his back pocket. His afternoon was booked with meetings with the engineering and design teams where they would present their updates to the platform. Drake expected to be wowed, but having seen some of the first drafts, he knew they had a long haul ahead of them.

As he reached for the conference room door handle, his cell phone buzzed. Drawing it from his pocket, the number and name leapt off his screen and stopped him mid-thought. Slowly, he swiped open the call.

"Hello, Allison?"

Natalie's mother's voice drifted out of his phone like soft waves on a lake at night.

"Hello, Drake. I hope I'm not interrupting you at work."

Drake looked through the windowed wall of the conference room at the team that had assembled and turned his back to them, while doing his best to re-focus on her call. *It had been months since he last spoke to her and it hadn't ended well. What could she possibly be calling him about now?*

"No, it's okay," He finally answered, "What can I do for you?"

"Well, hon, y'all been on my mind for a while now. Don told me to call you soona' but I simply couldn't gather up my nerves to do it."

Drake wasn't sure which shocked him more – the fact that she was calling him out of the blue or the fact that she had called him "hon."

"Well, okay," Drake spoke with a hushed voice so no one in the outer office area could hear him, "I thought you made it pretty clear when I was in Minnesota that you said all you had to say."

"Yes, that's right, I sho' did. But that was then. This is now. 'Sides Don says that I should come clean with y'all. He said it's high past time to do that."

"All right," Trying to prepare himself mentally for more shocking news about Natalie, Drake nodded as the last of the team members joining the meeting brushed past him into the conference room, "Let me go back to my office where I can-"

"No, Drake, not over the phone. Don and I are in Chicago, stayin' downtown, not too far from where you lived with Natalie. Do you still live there?"

"Yeah–"

"Could we meet you there this evenin'? Would that put you out too much?"

"Ah, no. That should be fine"

"Good. Let's say seven o'clock. We will see you then."

The hours between Allison's telephone call and his apartment buzzer announcing their arrival inched by with an excruciating inertia. After arriving home from the office and too anxious to eat dinner, he instead made a pot of coffee and tried to keep himself busy answering emails until the quiet condo seemed to fill with the sound of the buzzer at 7:10 pm.

They appeared to be dressed for dinner, although given the time, he expected that their reservation must be after this visit so hopefully, they would keep it short and to the point.

"Good evening, Allison," Drake said as cordially as he could muster and then nodded towards his ex-father-in-law, "Don. How have you been?"

"I've been good, Drake." Don reached for his hand and shook it warmly. Obviously, he intended to pretend that the words they'd said about him in the media over the years of Natalie's disappearance investigation hadn't happened.

"Well, that's good. Come on in. Could I offer you something to drink? I made coffee." Drake called over his shoulder as he headed towards the kitchen.

After a glance at Allison, who seemed extremely uncomfortable being here, Don spoke for them both as he helped Allison remove her expensive-looking black wool coat, revealing a glittery, rose-colored, silk blouse and a fitted silk skirt.

"That sounds perfect, thanks. Black is fine for me. Allison takes a shot of cream, if you have it."

"Okay. Just make yourselves comfortable, I will be right back." As he filled their cups, Drake tried to assess their body language as they sat stiffly on the couch facing the wall of windows overlooking the city.

Okay, he thought as he walked with the two cups towards them, *this is it. And it must be big, so prepare yourself.*

"So, what brings you guys to Chicago?" He asked with as much confidence as he could muster.

"Well, you remember my son, Nathan," Don was first to speak again while Allison sat quietly staring straight ahead out the window, "He recently opened a dental office in Schaumberg, so we decided to come out to visit."

Drake did remember Don's son from his first marriage. A little bit on the braggadocious side for his taste, but overall, Nathan seemed like a good guy.

"Oh? Well, good for him," Drake offered the small talk graciously, "I hope it's successful for him-"

"Drake," Allison interrupted, her gold dangle earrings fluttering in her hair as she snapped her head towards him, "let's all jus' cut through the meringue and git to the lemons-"

Drawing out the "ang" sound in meringue with an unusually harsh tone in her drawl, Allison's abrupt interruption and movement to the window surprised Drake so much he fumbled mentally with her lemon meringue pie metaphor for a moment. As he waited for her to continue, he watched her pace alongside the windows while Don sat in silent, languid observation, obviously not shocked by anything she was about to do or say.

"Don forced me to come tonight," She turned around with a hand on one hip and accused her husband, "I didn' wanna come. He *forced* me."

At the admission, Allison shot daggers from her genteel blue eyes towards her husband who, to his credit, sat stalwart on the couch, holding his ground, "But now that we're heah', let's just please git on with it."

"I know you been lookin' into the people Natalie knew in Minnesota," She continued, "Don't try to deny it, Dane already called me to tell me so. For the life of me, I don' know why you persist in this matta'. But since you are so obstinate, I figure I might as well tell you what I suspec'.

"I think I know who she mightta been meetin' that day she had her accident 'cause I have reason to believe this man was back in Minnesota. She met him when she was just a chile'. He was always more cunning than her, always up to no good.

"She was so innocent when she was young, she never meant to do it, I know it. That's why I wen' along with his proposal, y'see? I wanted to protect my baby."

Allison stopped talking then. Her eyes were misting as she glanced at Don and then bit her lip nervously before turning back to the window again.

Drake, totally confused by all the unspoken details of the story, looked from her to Don and then back again. After waiting for a long, patient moment, Drake realized that no one was going to offer any clarity unless prompted.

"I don't know what you're talking about, Allison. What – or whom – did she need protecting from?"

"From him. He knew her secret, she trusted him, she told him all about it and instead of doin' her right, he turned aroun' and threatened to use it against her. I always told her that man would be the death of her, but she wouldn't lissen..."

"Wh- what did she do?"

Allison turned to face him and with a last long glance at Don, she said clearly, "She killed her stepfather."

There had been many times in his personal and business life when Drake had been hit hard with unexpected news and he had become accustomed to the way his mind worked and his physical reaction in these situations. Most often, his mind would go numb for a moment, almost as if it was assessing the damage and then immediately it would fire back up again, ready to tackle the problem.

This. Was. Different.

Natalie killed her stepfather.

His mind was stuck on pause.

Or, maybe he misunderstood? Certainly, he couldn't have heard Allison correctly.

"What did you say?" The words were uttered from his lips, but he couldn't hear himself saying them until she answered, repeating the unbelievable.

"Natalie killed her stepfather when she was fourteen, she pushed him off the roof of our house. I wasn't home at the time and it turns out they were there alone. But I didn' know! She nevva told me the truth 'bout how he died. She let me believe that she wasn't there and that he fell to his death by accident."

"But, why? Why would she do such a thing?"

"Why would she lie or why would she kill 'im in the first place? You tell me 'cause she never would. And I could nevva ask her." Allison began to pace from one end of the windowed wall to the other as she continued, "It wasn't until later, after I collected on life insurance, that I heard from 'im, that dirty dawg. He said Natalie told 'im all about it and that he could make my life – and Natalie's – miserable unless I paid him to keep quiet. He said I committed insurance fraud and that Natalie would go to prison for what she did."

"But you haven't said why she did it in the first place." Drake forced the words out from the quicksand that he felt stuck in at that moment.

"I don' know why! He would never tell me, which has led me to think all kinds of God-awful things all these years. But he said if I ever told Natalie that I knew what happened, he would know I broke our deal, and he would go straight to the law. It was his way of controlling us both, y'see? He could blackmail me, and he could control her too because he had somethin' on her now. I have to believe that's why she went along with some of his schemes. He controlled my baby like a puppet."

"How long did this go on?"

"You mean the blackmail? It went on for years and years, ten or twenty thousand dollars at a time. He would contact me randomly, always wanted money wired to different bank accounts, I s'pose so I couldn' track 'im."

"When was the last time he contacted you?" Nothing about this was making sense to him as Drake struggled to put it into some perspective.

"See, that's what's strange. We were so confused after she stole the money from Rolph and then disappeared. Of course, we thought the worst - that Rolph had her killed or even – well, yes, we thought maybe you had done somethin' to her."

Drake swallowed hard to hear it come from her mouth, with Don sitting right in front of him. How they could have ever thought such a thing was completely unfathomable. Didn't they ever consider their son-in-law as a son, like his own parents considered his own sister's husband Caleb as a son? Did Allison and Don ever believe that he loved their daughter at all?

Allison ignored the insult she'd hurled at him and continued with her story.

"But then he contacted me twice more, so I tried to believe she had run away from Chicago and was with him somewhere. I think he was in Minneapolis that last time because he called me and pretended like he didn' know where she was, that he was looking for her. But I didn' believe 'im - I guess I thought he was with her. Now I know different. She was in the river."

Allison stopped speaking suddenly, pulled her lips together into a thin line and wiped at her eyes with the back of her finger.

"It's been a while now since we heard from him," Don spoke up from the couch, reminding Drake that he was there and had been a victim of this blackmail for many years too, "We think he might be in prison or something, thank God. I can't think of anything else that would stop that man."

Such a burden of secrets they had carried for years. And remembering the strain he'd always felt in their relationship, he wondered if Allison was being completely honest with him about Natalie's innocence in this scheme.

"Are you sure that Natalie didn't know about him blackmailing you? I know it's hard to think about, but maybe they were in it together?"

"As her mother, I don' wanna think so, but I s'pose it's possible." Allison conceded with a tired sigh as she joined Don on the couch again before continuing quietly, "Well, there you have what I've been supectin', Drake. I hope you feel better for the knowledge of it."

"Well, thank you for telling me. I admit, it's like drinking from a fire hose, but it does put some things into perspective. I've learned a lot about your daughter – my ex-wife - after looking deeper into her life. Basically, I've learned two things - nothing is what it seemed, and anything is possible."

There was no end to the number of secrets Natalie had kept. And look where they had gotten her, look at the people she had invited into her life.

Gradually, a picture was emerging in Drake's mind, it started as flashes of inspiration then became a dull haze of recognition. Maybe the "boy" she met as a young girl - the boy who grew into a man who would control her - had eventually become a DEA agent who now lived with a family in a quiet Minneapolis suburb.

Could Jeremy Hawthorne be the same man that had been blackmailing Allison and Don?

"Allison, what's this guy's name?"

"He went by Tony Carmine when she met 'im, but Natalie let it drop one time that he changed his name, maybe more than once."

"Did she ever say he went by Jeremy Hawthorne?"

"Ah, no, I don't think so, that doesn't ring a bell."

"Oh, okay. I just came across a guy named Jeremy Hawthorne who had been – tangled up with Natalie a few years back. I thought maybe it was the guy."

"Well-" Allison reached across the couch towards her expensive-looking leather bag and lifted a photograph from the front pocket. As he held his breath, Drake watched as she dropped it on the ottoman in front of him, allowing it to flutter unceremoniously downwards until it came to stop in front of him, "Does that look like 'im?"

Drake reached for the photo. It was grainy and water-stained, taken some time in the early 2000s, he guessed. He could make out a beautiful, blonde-haired, lanky girl with short shorts and a striped top leaning against a tall guy with wavy, dark hair. The man looked a few years older than her with his arm around her, drawing her against his side while she glanced up at his face, seemingly entranced. The hand that wasn't firmly gripping her waist was holding a beer bottle as he leaned against what looked like a bar at a beach-side restaurant, judging by the water visible behind it.

This was the guy who had captivated Natalie so completely that she would do anything he asked of her? This was the guy who she truly loved?

"I found it after one of her visits many years ago," Allison intruded on his thoughts, "She forgot some things at our house, and it was inside a bag she left. That's Tony Carmine, or TC as she called 'im. I call 'im the devil."

Drake looked at the picture again, even closer this time. He had similar dark hair, he had similar height. And if a DEA agent was willing to steal from the government agency he worked for and have an affair with his informant, he had similar criminal tendencies as Tony Carmine.

Yes. He could see how it all fit together.

Jeremy Hawthorne and Tony Carmine just might be the same guy.

CHAPTER 26

2014

Natalie

That December 15, the weather was unseasonably warm. Rolph's flight to New Orleans left on schedule that morning and I offered to drive him to the airport. He told me that he would try to call me that evening, but he had dinner plans with a client, so he wasn't sure what time.

I said, "No problem, sugar, you know where I will be – either at the office or home in bed missing my sweetheart."

He smiled a sappy smile and kissed me goodbye.

That was a completely normal workday, or at least I did my best to make it so. I had consciously developed a pattern of staying later than the rest of the office, sometimes until after the night cleaning crew left the office. Rolph had begun to accept that I worked late, even though he often complained that I worked later than he did.

That night, after everyone had left for the day, I went out to my car that I had parked near the side door, the one without a security camera, and brought the oversize cooler into the office. I had already disabled the cameras in the hallway and in Rolph's office earlier in the day and fixed it so that the settings would show the cameras low on battery charge, not fully disabled.

At this point, you might be asking, was I scared? Was I concerned that I would get caught?

A few times during the day, I would stop and ask myself those very same questions. I had walked through the scenarios so often in my head – what if someone else stayed overly late? What if someone came back because they forgot their cell phone or something? What if the cleaning crew changed their schedule? I had an answer for each scenario.

So, honestly, the answer was No, I wasn't scared I'd get caught.

This was a plan set in motion and I couldn't really turn back now anyway, even if I got cold feet. Besides, part of me really believed that I deserved the life that Rolph's ill-gotten gains could provide me.

As I packed the last of the money into the cooler and was about to roll it into the hallway on my way out the door, my cell phone rang. It was Rolph asking me if I was still at the office and wondering if everything was alright? It was so late, he said, and he was notified by the home security system app on his phone that the system hadn't been activated yet for the night. He was worried that I was home alone, and that I'd forgotten to set it.

TC always said the most believable lies are the ones with a good share of truth in them.

If I lied about where I was, Rolph would most likely know, so I told him the truth, just not the whole truth. As I sighed that it had been a long day and I was just leaving the office, I hefted the cooler into the back end of my SUV.

He told me that I worked too hard and when he got back to the office, he wanted to hire another person to lighten my load. That way, he said, I would have more time to spend with him.

I told him that he was the most generous man alive and that sounded heavenly.

A few minutes later, I was headed out of town when, euphoric with adrenaline, I dialed TC's burner phone to tell him everything had gone completely according to his plan.

That's when it all fell apart.

"Hello– who's this?" The tiny voice whispered on the other end of the phone, but it wasn't TC. This voice was innocent and scared, like a child hiding in a closet playing with his dad's phone. Which he obviously was.

I froze in shock at the sound of it.

"This is– a friend of–" I stuttered into the darkness trying to keep the car in between the lines on the road in front of me but it was hard to see through the hot tears that suddenly burned in my eyes. The truth burned even hotter through me.

TC had a son. This one he raised. This son he claimed.

"Do you have your daddy's phone?" I finally choked out the words, sure of what I'd hear.

"Yes, but daddy will be mad at me if he finds out."

There was the proof. His daddy.

I swallowed against the hurt that rose in my throat and something painfully shifted inside me. The memories of my pregnancy, the birth of our baby boy and the day I gave him away all flooded me, cutting me into a million pieces, like waves of shattered glass.

Too much. This was too much.

I blinked against the tears as I heard the breath of the little boy on the other end of the phone, waiting for me to say something.

"Then you'd better turn it off," I said quietly into the stillness, "Put it back where you found it and don't tell your daddy."

"Okay. I will-"

With a rustle and some loud clicks, the call suddenly broke off and my phone was silent again in my hand.

All my life I had detested men. I'd never seen redeeming qualities in them, I'd used them, I'd never trusted them.

Except TC. In some warped way, even after I witnessed the imbalance of power between us, I'd convinced myself that I could trust him because I thought he was brutally honest with me about everything.

Now, I saw clearly how he'd been using me because I was a woman and, even though he detested all people, he especially detested women. He'd never seen redeeming qualities in women, he'd used them, he needed to control them, and he'd never trusted them.

I thought I was different. I thought since I understood him, he would at least be honest with me, like I was with him. Instead, he had used me. Over and over again.

My entire life, he had used me.

Clear eyed now as I examined the hard truth of my life, I considered this most recent job with my husband, Rolph Sartell.

Who had sacrificed the most to do this job? Me.

Who had the most to lose? Me.

Who was carrying the money? Me.

Who could now change the plan – and not breathe a word about it to TC? Me.

Chapter 27

2019

Drake

He hadn't slept much at all the night before; thankfully, his morning run had gradually focused his mind and his spirit. Three days had gone by since Allison and Don's visit and still he hadn't made any contact with Detective Miller about the photo, even though it was in his possession now.

Although it meant she might be charged with insurance fraud, Allison had grudgingly agreed that he should contact the police. She said Don had convinced her and although she appeared to waver right before Drake's eyes, she overcame her fear and shoved the photo into his hands before they left.

"Go for it, hon. I'm done runnin' from that devil." She said and then they walked out, heads held high, most likely never to appear in Drake's life ever again.

His first reaction was to call Detective Miller immediately. But as he prayed about it, Drake found himself waiting. Not exactly sure why he felt the need to wait, he spent the past three days studying scripture and stories of patience and eternal perspective found in the Bible. In each of these, the message was clear – Seek ye first the kingdom of God.

He found himself reflecting again on his life and calling out the areas where he had skewed the importance of worldly matters over the matters of God.

His business. Natalie. The demise of their marriage. Natalie's disappearance. The despair over being a suspect. The almost-fatal decline of his business. The regrowth of his business. The confirmation of Natalie's death. And now this quest of his to figure it out.

All of it, each one of these, had teetered precariously on the edge of idolatry. As he lived through each of these phases, each had become his identity. Each became the way he thought of himself, the way he defined himself.

And by doing that, it meant he had not really defined himself "in Christ." His priorities had been off.

When he had his priorities in order, it was clear to him that this life was temporary. It was all leading up to that moment when he would stand before his heavenly Father. And, if there was one thing that he was sure of, when he finished this race called life and he met his maker, he wanted to hear the words, "Well done, good and faithful servant."

Clarity. He felt it slice through him. A flash of consciousness that he often sought, this time was spontaneously delivered, and obligated prompt action.

Determined to conquer this quest once and for all, Drake reached for his cell phone and thumbed through his contacts as he searched for Detective Miller's number.

Drawing in a breath as the phone rang, he let it out abruptly as a voice mail picked up.

"You've reached Detective Miller's phone," The familiar, gruff voice announced, "I have been reassigned to another unit so if you have information on a case, please contact Detective Juarez by calling the precinct office. Thanks."

Huh.

Okay, now what? Should he really go through all this with a new detective? And which detective would it be anyway? Missing persons? Stolen property? Homicide?

Then, another thought came to mind. Maybe he should call Sheriff Cooper in Twin Shores? As far as Drake knew, he was still investigating the discovery of Natalie's body in his county. He could mail or scan the photo and email it to the sheriff – who knows, maybe they would need him to come back to Minnesota for a statement.

Drake tried not to think about how his stomach fluttered with the thought of seeing Gisella again.

After finding the website for the sheriff's department on the internet, he dialed the number and sipped from his steaming coffee cup as he waited for someone to pick up.

"Hi, Sheriff's office, Twin Shores." A woman answered brusquely, all-business in a distinctly Minnesotan accent.

"Ah, yes. Is Sheriff Cooper in today, please?" Drake said and then noticed a notification on his phone that he was receiving another call.

Gisella.

Gisella?

Going to voice mail.

Drake frowned in frustration at the timing of missing her call as he heard the woman on the other end of the line say, "Please hold, I will hunt down the sheriff and get him on the phone for ya'."

CHAPTER 28

November 2019

Drake and Sella

"Drake, thanks so much for returning my call-" Returning her call a few minutes later, Drake strained to hear Gisella as she spoke with halted words and in such a hushed tone that Drake checked the volume on his cell phone before pressing it closer against his ear.

The volume on his phone was normal. It was her voice that wasn't normal and the hairs on his neck bristled with slow dread.

"Of course," He replied with concern, "what is it, Gisella? Is something wrong?"

"He's gone, Drake," She stated in a flat, colorless declaration, "My dad. He died last night."

As she relayed more details, the hurt poured through the cell phone and tore his heart out. Listening to her strained voice, as she struggled not to cry, Drake felt her pain physically. Finally, as she brought the call to an end, he heard her cry, almost like the whimper of a lost child.

As he said goodbye, he gripped his phone tightly in his hand, surprising himself with the intensity of his emotional response. While Gisella sat alone in Minnesota mourning the loss of a father who meant everything to her, he sat hours away in Chicago, unable to take her in his arms, unable to comfort her in any way.

It took a few minutes of reflection on why he was reacting the way he was, but gradually, Drake recognized something.

Something about Gisella and something about himself. And it was big.

Two days later, Drake was on the interstate leading away from the airport, headed toward northern Minnesota to attend a funeral for a man that only a few months ago he hadn't known existed but now he felt was part of his family.

Luca had a stroke. In her phone call, Gisella told him that it happened during the night and that Luca had passed quickly. She said that there were so many miserable things about the timing of his death – it happened in his bed in her home and so suddenly that no one had time to say goodbye – but the saddest part was that Henri had found him when he went to wake him that morning. Luca was laying peacefully still, with one leg outside of the covers as if he had started to rise but then just laid down again and shut his eyes forever.

Such a typically mundane thing to do she said, as confusion and shock reverberated in her voice, it was just part of the daily, morning routine - "Go in and wake up Poppy."

Instead of rousing him from sleep, Henri found his grandpa and best friend gone forever. The shock of it was devastating for Henri, she said, and they were both in denial, still struggling to comprehend what had happened.

Of course, Drake was concerned about Henri and he told Gisella so, but he was also worried about her. She seemed so strong, always the one everyone relied upon. But, with her brothers all grieving with spouses and families of their own, Drake wondered, who would be there for her?

The question brought him back to the revelation he had the day she called. The longer he allowed himself to consider it, in fact, the clearer that revelation became.

He was falling in love with Gisella. Or maybe he was already way past that and was already deeply in love with her. Time would tell, he supposed. Time ... and her reaction when he told her how he felt. That would impact it as well.

He hoped her response wouldn't break his heart.

***

The heavy clouds reflected Drake's mood that morning as he arrived at the church and searched for an empty parking spot in the overflowing lot.

As he joined the group of people walking somberly towards the church, he pulled his coat's collar up and ducked his head to avoid the gusty winds and pelting, ice-slivered rain. Stepping past the last row of cars, Drake noticed a sheriff's car parked across the street which reminded him that Sheriff Cooper would be here today and that he could now hand-deliver the photo that he'd brought along with him from Chicago.

Maybe he had misjudged his demeanor on the phone, but the other day Drake had been disappointed when the sheriff told him that the investigation had gone cold and the mention of the photo hadn't even seemed to pique his interest. Resisting the temptation to give up, Drake hoped seeing him in person would inspire a bit more enthusiasm from the sheriff.

Entering the church lobby, Drake was surprised to see that the sanctuary was already at capacity and additional chairs were being set up in the lobby area to accommodate last minute arrivals. Amazed at such a turn-out on a day with such miserable weather, it was obvious that each community that hosted a Lafayette Autos location was well represented and the turn-out was a testament to the impact Luca Lafayette had on so many.

Drake searched the sea of faces for Gisella and Henri, but he could not find anyone he recognized amongst the crowd. As he was ushered to an empty seat near the far side of the church, he ruminated on the aching sadness in the faces of people around him.

Luca Lafayette had been an institution in these communities. If anything, as he passed into his old age, his influence had been extended even further as his children built a local rapport with the towns' residents.

And even though Luca was probably now rejoicing in heaven, the church at that moment was full of mourning.

A few minutes later, Drake glanced up from the printed obituary to see the family entering the church sanctuary. Gisella and Henri were first in line, with Gisella's brother Phillip and his family following closely behind. As the rest of the family filtered into the benches at the front of the church, Drake watched as Gisella sighed heavily, drew Henri closer to her side and rested her head on her son's as the music for the first hymn drew to a close.

With so many people between them, from across the church Drake could just barely see her profile, but as her brother Phillip rose to read the eulogy a few minutes later, she wiped at her eyes with a tissue and smiled encouragingly at him as he stood behind the lectern.

Each of the three sons Phillip, Sebastian and Reese would take their place behind the lectern and shared stories of Luca's full-throated embrace of his faith in God, his keen sense of humor and the light of his life, his wife and his family along with the many friends he'd developed through his business.

Although the stories they shared engaged the audience, it was when Gisella took her place up front that he felt the audience sit up with undivided attention. She was so graceful in her delivery and so authentic in her words as she spoke of his everyday kindness to people in the church and community and all the small things that she would miss with him like their walks by the river, getting him dinner while he watched Wheel of Fortune on television, bringing him to the store so he could have coffee with "the guys."

She said, "I think of all these moments as the everyday minutia of life that, without knowing it, we were adding to the memory book of Dad's life. And, now that he's gone, it's the memory book that we have left to help fill this gaping hole we feel now. I hope that I've stored up enough in that memory book to keep his memory alive for years to come. I love you dearly and will miss you so much, Poppy."

As he watched her from his seat near the back of the church, where he sat amongst complete strangers, Drake's heart ached for her. It was more than sympathy that he felt for her, it was a wrenching pain.

After the service, as he stood in the corner of the lobby, he watched her greet people and he noted the expression of robotic emptiness in her eyes. That remorseful expression didn't change, even as she tried to smile as people shared memories of her father with her.

Gisella's eyes were the window to her soul, no doubt. And it was obvious her soul was untethered and adrift today.

Drake followed the line of cars to the cemetery and again stood off at a distance as the family laid their father, grandfather and beloved friend to rest, next to his wife Violet.

As the members of her family and friends wandered slowly back to their cars, Drake found a moment when Gisella was alone. She stood by the casket, one hand resting lightly on top of it, as if she didn't want to let them take him away, as the other hand brushed tears away from her eyes. Her shoulders were shaking as she cried, and Drake didn't even try to stop the tears that were flooding his eyes as he watched her.

Not thinking twice, he joined her at the casket, reached out for her arm and turned her towards him slowly. She may have been startled to see him, but if she was, her surprise was quickly overwhelmed by a small, shaking smile.

"You came." She said, her voice cracking slightly with emotion as new tears glistened in the beautiful eyes that reminded him of autumn.

"Of course," He replied quietly as he opened his arm to her, "Gisella, I'm so sorry." He spoke into her soft hair, dampened by the mist in the air, as she laid her head on the front of his shoulder.

"I know. I'm sorry too," She nodded as she spoke into his wool coat, "We're just going to miss him so much."

"Yes, you will," Drake agreed, "He's the kind of guy that everyone misses, especially those who know him best and love him the most."

"Yeah. I know it will get easier," She continued, as if trying to rationalize the grieving while her shoulders shook with her sobs, "but right now, it's really, really hard."

"Mhmm." Drake nodded and tightened his arms around her, giving her support as she shook against his chest.

Showing his "soft side" emotions had never been a strength of his. It was true that he had always been a very emotional guy – he was the one who led the charge, cheered people on, he felt emotions deeply and always had – but showing his vulnerabilities, showing how painful life could be sometimes? That was not something he was comfortable doing.

Unless he felt *very comfortable* with someone.

Unless he felt *very committed* to someone.

Like he felt with Gisella.

So, he let the tears flow freely and hugged her even tighter, never wanting to let her go.

Sella

"I'm glad you decided to stay in town, Drake. Yesterday was such a blur, I'm sure I missed thanking lots of people for their support." Sella was pleasantly surprised when she saw his call come in the following morning and that he had made the extra effort to contact her again after the funeral.

The lengthy, emotional funeral left her mind and body drained of all energy as she dragged herself home last evening, feeling like she had just barely finished a grueling marathon race with enough energy to breathe.

She woke this morning in a slightly less foggy state, and while sitting in front of the fire drinking a cup of tea and reading her Bible, she felt her spirit renewed with each passage that she read.

"I can imagine the day was tough for you," Drake's voice was smooth and kind, prompting her to miss the smile she knew was always quick to end up on his mouth, "There were so many people who loved Luca, I'm sure you are completely wiped out from it all."

"Well, it has been a lot to take in. Hard to fathom that it's been less than a week since Henri found him that morning." She said as her voice trailed off sadly, remembering anew that awful morning and Henri's reaction.

"How is Henri doing, by the way?" Drake wondered aloud, "I saw him with his cousins yesterday and they seemed to be getting on with it the way kids do."

"He's coming along, better each day, I guess. He's staying at Phillip's house this weekend. I think it's good for him to be with kids right now. It's just too quiet here and too many reminders of his Poppy."

"Good idea." Drake said solemnly, then seemed to rush on before taking a breath, "My flight out isn't until tomorrow, Gisella. Could we see each other before I leave? Maybe you could show me one of those hiking trails you guys talked about?"

"Okay, sure, but you'd better dress warm it gets cold in the woods," She replied, wondering belatedly if she had the energy to do a hike. But she couldn't help noticing the flutter his invitation brought to her stomach - how could she turn his invitation down? "Would you like to come over in about an hour? I could make a lunch and then we could go."

"You got it - on my way out the door right now." His voice sounded like the smile that she longed to see as he hung up the phone.

Sella laughed slowly as she glanced at her phone and closed out the call. Not quite sure what to think, she suspected he had news on Natalie's disappearance by the way he was acting. If that was the case, she was happy for him. She'd always wanted him to get some kind of resolution with his quest, as he called it.

But, honestly, part of her still wanted more from Drake than this friendship they had developed. And no one was more surprised at her realization of this than she was.

Even though it had ended amicably between them, dating Zachary Wyler for a few weeks had opened her eyes to a whole new life. She felt attractive and accessible – not in a desperate, wanton way, but in a level-headed, open-hearted way that she hadn't felt since Garrett left her.

And this fluttering in her stomach at the prospect of seeing Drake alone for a few hours? To her that was confirmation that her open-heart was beating again.

***

They rounded the bend of the trail as the sunlight sliced through the birch sending haphazard prisms of light over them. Seeing a group of large boulders alongside the trail in some welcome sunlight, Drake hobbled over to them, breathed in the sharp pine fragrance of the trees surrounding them as he leaned against the rocks and gulped from his water bottle.

"No way. You mean we're still not done with this trail? I need to stop for a moment-" He laughed as he wiped his mouth before the crisp breeze could turn his lips numb.

"Sure, no problem. I can see you're a novice, I don't mind going slow." Laughing at all his drama, Gisella joined him at the boulder, leaning into it for support against her back.

They had talked a lot about her dad over lunch and how her dad's passing was affecting Henri. Sella was reminded again by how thoughtful Drake was, coming all the way from Chicago for her dad's funeral and caring so much about how they were adjusting.

Then as they started their hike, he'd begun to tell her about the visit from Natalie's parents and the crazy story of Natalie secret involvement in her stepfather's death and the man who held it over her for years. Sella was completely floored by all of it and the eventual blackmail of Natalie's mother seemed straight out of a made-for-TV movie. Stuff like that just didn't happen to people she knew.

With a sense of tired relief, Drake told her that he'd finally reached the end of his quest. He said he even planned to meet with Coop later that afternoon to review with him all that he'd learned and hoped that somehow Coop could find the man and hold him accountable.

The relief was evident in Drake's voice and Sella could feel the optimism in his whole demeanor. Even given her heavy mood, with reminders of her dad all around her in these woods, Sella felt good for Drake – *she was really happy for him.*

As she perched her sunglasses on top of her head, Sella was about to tell him how good she felt for him, when she noticed his vibrant blue eyes were suddenly extra-intense and his face was serious, the flirty grin that usually turned up his mouth was gone and he regarded her carefully.

"Gisella, I've been thinking," He started, then the smile returned, his face softening again into a full, sheepish grin, "Great, now that I want to tell you, I can't think of the words-"

He waited, watching her for a moment longer, as she held her breath, not exactly sure where this was going but breathlessly excited to find out.

"I know that the distance between us isn't ideal," He continued as he held her gaze steadily, not wavering, "But I'm wondering, have you ever felt anything for me?"

What was he talking about? Sella fumbled around inside her head. She didn't want to make the embarrassing assumption he meant romantically, because if he didn't mean that... well, that would be a moment that she couldn't possibly recover from.

But the way he was looking at her ...

"You mean, as more-" She started to say, slightly frustrated that he was making her verbalize something that he, after all, had started to say.

"Yeah, more." He agreed quickly as if not wanting her to continue with the trite "more than a friend" phrase.

She faltered, now that it was clear what he meant, her brain locked on pause and she was unable to form words.

In the absence of her reply, he continued, "I have feelings for you, Gisella. I can't seem to get you out of my mind. I think about you all the time and I want to get to know you more. As in – you know, more." He laughed then and looked down at his feet with a sheepish smile, as if he decided it was best to stop talking.

It was a step, she thought to herself. *Something that people did every day. They didn't always know where they were going and where that step would take them. They just took it.*

And, so should she.

"Well. More sounds – good." Sella said softly, still a little unsure of what she was saying. She reached out towards him, resting her palm against the back of his hand on the rock surface between them.

"Okay, that's great!" Drake said, clearly relieved, his head bobbing up with a smile. He took her hand into his as he gazed down at it, "I wasn't sure if you and the deputy were an 'item.'"

"Ah, no," Sella smiled at his enthusiasm, "Zachary is a great guy and everything, but I didn't feel – well, I didn't feel *like that* about him."

This left it abundantly clear that she felt "like that" about Drake and her cheeks fired at the obvious implications of her statement.

"Okay," His eyes crinkled into a smile as he caught the meaning, "Well, that's good. I know that it's not the best timing for me to tell you all this - what with your dad and everything - and I know you need time to let everything settle in. I just wanted you to know how I felt before I left town."

"Drake, I'm glad you told me," Sella smiled, feeling herself loosen up as she linked her fingers with his, "But, you should know, it takes me a while to warm up to things sometimes. The idea of someone else – well, it's been a long time since I've felt that way about anyone."

"I know, me too," He agreed, and it set her ease, "But, with you, something's different. I suspected it when I was here before, but now - coming back here – I'm sure of it."

"But you don't really know me, Drake," Sella persisted, feeling it was really important for him to understand early on just how unpracticed she was at relationships, "I'm not the touchy-feely kind of person you are and I'm certainly nothing like Natalie from the sounds of it."

"Oh, so I'm touchy-feely, huh?" He teased as he pulled her arm closer to his side and then let her loose again, "And you think – after all I've learned about my ex-wife – that I would want someone like that ever again? Gisella, come on. You know that sounds crazy."

"Well, I just want you to see-" She continued, belaboring her point.

"Listen," Drake interrupted her, silencing her with his intense gaze, "what I *see* is a beautiful, Godly woman, a wonderful mother, and someone who is unique and precious. Your roots go deep, Gisella. That's what I see."

***

It was a state of euphoria he hadn't experienced since – well, ever. He felt like the luckiest man alive! As he pulled his rental car into the parking lot of the sheriff's department later that afternoon, Drake glanced into the rear-view mirror to see if it was obvious all over his face.

Wow, he was falling fast. If Gisella had any idea, it could be dangerous.

After his meeting with Sheriff Cooper, he planned to take her out to one of the nicest restaurants in the area to "wine and dine her," as his father would say. It wasn't meant to simply impress her, although that would be nice, it was more to show her how much he cared for her. Even though he'd known her now for a few months, he'd never actually been on a date with her.

And a real date was long overdue.

A buzzer sounded as the door opened and he was greeted by the smell of overcooked coffee. A large, hulking man who strained the chest and sleeves of his uniform, Sheriff Cooper stood at the coffee pot behind the front desk, pouring himself a cup. He smiled with familiarity as he recognized Drake from their short visit at the funeral the other day.

"Hello, Drake. Thanks for coming in." Sheriff Cooper said, then offered him a cup, "You want some coffee?"

"No, thanks. I'm good."

"Okay, let's head back to my office."

They walked the short corridor and entered a sparsely decorated office with a simple wooden desk and filing cabinets along a wall underneath some over-size prints of the sheriff and what looked like his family - a wife and two kids - on fishing trips.

"You like to fish, I see." Drake commented as he sat down in a chair across the desk from the large man.

"Yes, my wife is a professional guide." He said proudly as he nodded towards a photo of a pretty, red-haired woman with her hair tied back under a Cabela's hat, holding a huge walleye.

"Nice."

"She is," No offense to the sheriff's wife, but Drake had been talking about the fish. Obviously, Sheriff Cooper misunderstood as he gazed in admiration at his wife, "She's a keeper, that's for sure."

After a moment's pause, the sheriff continued, a cool tone soaking through his deep baritone voice, "So, Drake, you mentioned on the phone why you showed up here this past summer, most of which I already knew-"

"Oh? How did you know?"

"Phillip Lafayette told me. It's a small town and a stranger showing up asking questions about a local incident isn't something we're used to seeing every day." The sheriff said, and even though it was awkward that the two men had been talking about Drake and his motives for being here, nothing about the sheriff's demeanor said he felt bad about it, "Plus, he's - we - all are pretty protective of Sella."

That statement might have rankled Drake a few months ago, but now he was glad to hear it. He could understand why.

"Good," Drake answered honestly, shifting in his chair slightly, "I'm glad."

"Okay, good, we're straight on that," The sheriff stated evenly. Obviously comfortable being the one in control, he leveled his light-eyed gaze at Drake, "So, then, you'd also understand why I did some extra digging into you and the suspicions law enforcement had of you at one time."

"Yes, and you found that they've cleared me of any involvement with Natalie's disappearance."

"You're right. But it does seem a bit odd that you would continue to pursue these questions about her, once we found her car. I'm not saying what you've learned won't be helpful to us, it may well be, but it does seem odd. Most people don't go around looking to be involved with police investigations."

"I wasn't involved with the police," Drake explained, wanting his motives to be as transparent as possible, "I was just asking questions of family and friends of my ex-wife. I was curious, I guess. The information wasn't hard to find once I started asking some questions."

"Well, I took notes on the people you told me about over the phone and we will follow up," Sheriff Cooper said, as he sat forward slightly in his chair, "So now, you mentioned you have a photo of the man you suspect was involved with Natalie just before she went missing?"

"Yes, I'm thinking it's the DEA agent I told you about but the photo is really old and it's hard to make out his features-" Drake removed the photo from his back pocket and pressed down the curled corners so Sheriff Cooper could get a good look.

"What the-" Shifting closer to the photo, Sheriff Cooper stopped his sentence, removed the reading glasses that were nestled in his front shirt pocket and once he set them on his nose, he peered more closely at the picture. Dropping his mouth open, he frowned at Drake, his light eyes taking on a hard, darkened glint, "Wait. Tell me again, who did you think this man is?"

"I'm thinking it may be Agent Jeremy Hawthorne and I have his number. I found his address in Bloomington."

"But you're not *sure* it's him. No one *confirmed* for you that this man is Jeremy Hawthorne." He spoke to the picture, not raising his gaze toward Drake.

"Well, ah, no, I guess I can't say with certainty that it's him."

As he watched the sheriff dissect the photo, Drake's mind spun in circles; he had been so sure of his theory that he missed the main point - he wasn't absolutely sure of the man's identity because only two people could confirm it.

Natalie and her mother.

One was dead and he hadn't taken the time to show the other a recent photo of Jeremy Hawthorne to confirm this was him.

Drake, sensing the initial whispers of defeat seeping into his spirit again, questioned slowly, "Why do you ask me if I can confirm it?"

"Because I know who this man is," Sheriff Cooper uttered and then bent his eyes towards the photo again, shock evident across his face, "and his name isn't Jeremy Hawthorne and he doesn't live in Bloomington."

Chapter 29

November 2019

Sella

Music followed her down the hallway from her bathroom as Sella returned to the kitchen to retrieve her cell phone from her charger. She wasn't sure how long his meeting with Coop would take, but if Drake tried to text her, she wanted to make sure she saw it.

Mariah Carey's Christmas CD was the featured music tonight at the local radio station, which usually played a mix of light rock, but was already sprinkling in Christmas music during the evenings. She had been consciously trying to prepare herself for the grief they would all feel this first holiday season without her dad, and Christmas music sure wasn't helping. With a determined swipe, she switched the station.

There will be many moments to feel grief - but for now, tonight, I want to be thoroughly happy. I know dad would want that for me too.

Smiling to her reflection in her bathroom mirror, she swept her bangs back from her eyes and applied the last of her mascara. Then, adding a spritz of perfume, she switched the light off and returned to the kitchen to wait.

He should be here any minute, she thought as she pulled a chair away from the counter and sat down, drumming her fingers in anticipation on the marble countertop. She felt like a teenager waiting for her first date to arrive. She'd forgotten how much fun it could be, waiting for a date to arrive.

He drove up her driveway a few minutes later, perfectly punctual. Although it was rather gloomy outside with a light freezing drizzle, from the glow of the front porch lights, Sella could see him open his car door and stretch out from his car. Her stomach did another turn when he glanced towards the house and seemed to take a deep breath, almost bracing himself, she thought.

Why that look, she wondered. Something must not have gone well at the sheriff's department. Maybe they were angry with him for interfering in the investigation?

Sella had become concerned that Drake might inadvertently mess up the investigation by talking so freely to those he thought were involved with Natalie's disappearance. Perhaps Coop had told him that was a problem.

Well, no matter, she reasoned. If Coop had given him a hard time about interfering with the case, and he was feeling beaten down about that, then she would have to help lift Drake's spirits and divert his attention away from his long-gone ex-wife.

Natalie was Coop's problem now, she thought as she reached for the door handle.

"Hello, right on time!" She said as she pulled open the door and the sleet-heavy, icy air seeped into the cozy, fire-warmed entryway, making her shiver.

"Hi." He said, a weak smile of appreciation lighting his teary eyes as he appraised her darkened denim tunic dress, black tights and knee-high black leather boots.

Sella could tell he thought she looked nice, but his watery blue eyes and every other bit of his body language was screaming a completely different message.

"Drake, what is it?" She reached for his arm and ushered him into the house before closing the door behind him.

He stood still, completely immobile, and watched her from a few feet away. His lips moved and then stopped, then moved again, but nothing came out.

Finally, he turned away from her and rubbed his eyes roughly, as if the tears she saw in them were burning hot embers he could brush away and forget whatever news prompted them in the first place.

"What is it? You're freaking me out right now. Did something happen?" She couldn't help the slicing edge to her voice, she hated surprises. *And this didn't look like a good one.*

"Gisella. Oh, God. I can't even-" Still not looking at her, he slid his arms out of his coat, dropped in on the chair near the door and paced towards the fireplace, his back to her.

"Drake. *Please.* Tell me what's wrong."

Turning around to face her, he took in a deep breath and then, exhaling his breath in ragged shakes, Drake walked towards her and took her warm hands into his ice-cold ones.

"I need to tell you something. But you need to sit down."

As he led her towards the couch, Sella followed, dumbstruck. *What could possibly have happened for him to act this way?*

Once seated next to him, Drake held her hands with his head bowed, as if he was praying. But it was a silent prayer and when he looked up, it seemed that God had not answered it immediately because his eyes were bottomless wells of pain.

"I know who Natalie was planning to meet here in Minnesota."

"Really?" Inside Sella breathed a sigh of relief. This was what had him so emotional? But his reaction confused her; this was what he wanted to know, after all. It had to reach a conclusion at some point.

As soon as the thought went through her mind, she felt awful for treating his despair so casually. Carefully, she phrased her response to avoid hurting him further, "But, that's what you wanted to know, right, Drake? That was the whole point in you coming here in the first place, right?"

Sella squeezed his fingers, trying her best to encourage him.

"Yes, but not this. Not *him*." He looked back into her eyes and then, as if he couldn't bear to hold her gaze, he looked down again and stared at her hands holding his.

"Well, who is he? Is he from around here?"

At her question, his body went rigid still and he was so quiet it seemed he wasn't even breathing. Across the living room in the fireplace, a small log spit flames high into the chimney as it fell deeper into the glowing embers, capturing Sella's momentary attention.

Turning back to Drake, she watched breathlessly as he slowly raised his tortured gaze towards her and reached into the front pocket of his jeans. Retrieving a photograph, he held it front side down for a moment and then turned it over, holding it in his palm for her to see.

A pretty, blonde girl in a cute summer outfit looked up lovingly at a handsome, dark-haired man who stood by a beachside bar with water in the background.

Sella stopped breathing. Her trembling fingers reached for the photo in a motion as slow as the comprehension that was permeating through her consciousness.

She knew the smile, she knew the high, strong cheekbones, she had traced the scar on the front of the man's forearm hundreds of times, she knew the dark, wavy hair, silky like a mink's coat when you filtered your fingers through it, she knew the touch of his lips on hers and the rich timbre of his voice as he whispered *Good morning, love ...*

"Impossible. This is impossible-" Her voice cracked the silence. She knew she spoke, but she wasn't expecting anyone to answer. She felt completely alone in the room.

Alone. Again.

But she wasn't alone.

She was sitting alongside the man whose ex-wife had been having an affair with her husband.

"This is-" She started to say it again.

Impossible. This was impossible.

But was it?

Garrett had been gone so often and for such long periods of time, of course, she had suspected affairs.

But to be involved with someone like Natalie? A criminal like Natalie?

Impossible.

Garrett was her husband. He was the father of their son. He couldn't possibly have hidden something like this from her.

A whole separate life?

A criminal life?

Impossible.

Slowly, Sella raised her eyes to the man sitting next to her. She saw what looked like pain in his eyes - but seeing the world completely different now after seeing the photo - Sella was sure this look of "pain" had to be an act.

After all, what did she really know about this stranger named Drake Connor? How long had he known that Natalie and Garrett had been having an affair? Had he suspected from the beginning? Why had he been so persistent with getting to know her and her family, insinuating himself in their lives, earning their trust.

Winning their love.

Winning her love.

A fury fanned by wounded pride and sorrow lit up her torso and erupted onto her neck with a burning sensation as tears sprung onto her lashes.

"Get. Out." Sella spat the two words at him and pushed his hands away as if they were diseased.

"What- no, Gisella, please!" He was shocked by her response, but everything about him seemed phony now. He couldn't possibly be as shocked as he looked.

He had to have suspected something. There was no way he couldn't have known that Garrett was having an affair with his ex-wife.

He was some kind of sicko, coming here and using them in this way. And to think she had trusted him.

She had actually started to fall in −

No.

"I don't know what kind of sick game you've been playing, Drake, but I am done being your pawn in it," Sella sliced the words out in anger, building steam as she went along, "I never want to see you again or talk to you again. And, if I ever see you contact Henri again, I'm calling Coop. You understand me?"

Sella propelled herself up from the couch and stumbled towards the other side of the room, her legs unsteady and her head throbbing with a sudden headache that seemed to split her skull into two parts.

"Gisella−" Drake stood quickly and stepped after her with his arms outstretched towards her.

"*Don't call me that,*" She spat again, hiccupping over the tears that filled her throat and tumbled from her eyes. Grabbing his coat as she passed the chair where he'd left it, she threw the coat at him roughly, "Don't even talk to me. Just get out or I'm calling Coop right now."

Still stumbling away from him, she finally stopped in the far corner of the room, cowering there with her arms crossed over her chest, not wanting to feel his presence anywhere near her.

Rationally, she recognized her threats were bluster; she knew she had nothing to fear from him physically.

But, still, she knew she had a lot to be fearful of when it came to Drake Connor. She had trusted him, even after fighting it at first, she had trusted him. With her life, with her son's life. With her heart.

He had done a number on her alright.

When she looked up again, he was gone.

CHAPTER 30

December 2014

Natalie

About two hours later, after I'd worked out my plan in my head, I called TC.

I lied to him. I told him that it all went perfectly and that I was on my way to Detroit, when instead, I was making my way west across Wisconsin towards Minnesota.

That was about as much of a plan as I had at that moment. Find him, confront him, and make him decide which it would be – me and the money or the lie he was living with her and their family.

I drove through the night, fueled by adrenaline and caffeine. About half-way there, the snow started falling. At first it came down in light puffs that would glance off my windshield and over the roof of my car, but that was soon replaced by sheets of white that would come so heavy at times my wipers couldn't keep the windshield clear.

As I searched for weather reports on my car radio, I debated about stopping and riding the storm out in a hotel. But as the thought would cross my mind, I would tell myself, just keep going. You need to see the look on his face when you confront him. The anticipation of seeing him squirm – seeing him forced to choose - was more motivation than riding out the blizzard in the safety of a hotel.

It was morning. But I couldn't tell that by the sky because the sun was completely shrouded in snow. It didn't really matter to me because I had lost track of time over a hundred miles ago. After loading his address into my GPS many miles before, I knew roughly where I was going and arriving in the morning during a blizzard seemed to me like the perfect surprise attack.

As my stomach rumbled, I thought derisively, maybe they'd invite me to have breakfast with them. Wouldn't that be cozy?

My eyes were twitching with exhaustion and my shoulders were so knotted up I was losing sensation in my hands. As I passed a restaurant in Twin Shores, I glanced longingly at the lighted sign. I was so hungry and there must be people there because the sign was lit up. As I passed, though, I didn't see any cars. Even the locals didn't venture out in this weather.

It didn't matter if I was hungry anyway. I had to keep going. Not much further.

He lived deep in the woods, and the roads leading to his house were winding and remote. Judging by the snow on the road, it appeared that it hadn't been plowed since the blizzard began yesterday. Many times, I'd have to speed up to barrel through two and sometimes three-foot drifts across the road and each time my car would lose footing on the glare ice hidden below.

I couldn't see anything in the white and often I found myself hypnotized by silvery-white prisms of snow as they pummeled my windshield. More than once, I'd glance out my side window and be startled to find myself on the wrong side of the road.

That's when I noticed my hands were clammy. That's when the fear crept in.

I thought, wasn't it ironic that I could steal a million dollars without fear but being left alone in the woods in a white-out blizzard scared me senseless.

Suddenly, however, recognizing this fear in me made me mad — even madder than I was at TC - and I stepped on the gas. In exasperation, I glanced again at my GPS. Two miles to my destination. I had to keep going. This would all be over soon.

That's when I saw it. The dark monster sliced through the white as he charged at me from the driver's side of my car, a flurry of snow swirling around his massive, mud-brown body and light-colored antlers.

I swung the wheel to avoid the massive buck, and without realizing it, I closed my eyes in panic. When I opened them again, I saw nothing but swirling snow as my car swung round and round on the ice-caked road.

I held my breath as my car lifted into the air, turning in an impossible rotation.

Through my whipped hair and the scattered contents of my purse, I peered through the windshield in disbelief as I watched my car pitch nose-down through a wall of white.

Was I landing in a lake? I hadn't seen a lake on the GPS.

The noise of my car crunching in against me was deafening. The sight of the dark water was horrifying. The pain of my legs being snapped like twigs was debilitating and the gush of the blood from my head wound was sticky and thick.

But it was the fear of death that overwhelmed me. The fear of my imminent death was ... final.

Dark, cold and final.

CHAPTER 31

November 2019

Sella

The water trickled through her shaking fingers and down her face, dripping an inky black river of eyeliner residue from her chin into the sink below. Raising her head to look at her reflection in the mirror, Sella frowned in disgust at the sight of her tear-stained, blotchy face with its remnants of mascara shadowing under her bloodshot eyes.

You are so stupid.

She reached into the flow of water again and rubbed her cheeks raw as if somehow the action could remove the memory of how happy she had been just an hour ago.

How could you be so stupid?

Resting her hands against the vanity, Sella leaned into it, exhausted, and let the water and her tears run down her face and onto her neck, where they pooled on the towel that she had wrapped around herself after a cold shower.

Her husband had lied to her about everything. Every single thing.

So overwhelmed by the deluge of information that single photo had downloaded on her, Sella had lost her sense of time and rational thought, with the exception of one: Henri.

She was glad Henri was safe at her brother's house for the weekend. She wasn't sure how she could have ever respected herself again if he had been here to witness the truth about his father and the collapse of his mother.

Even as she prayed that God would intervene and impose on her a strength to resist the temptation, she struggled to find someone to blame for the dizzying waves of emotion that left her breathless and unable to think clearly.

She couldn't help but blame Drake. Here was a man who seemed so naïve to his ex-wife's secret, criminal life but had somehow just happened to stumble onto the spouse of the "other man." That seemed almost laughably implausible.

But the real predator had resided closer to her heart for a lot longer and the bite was much deeper. Her husband Garrett- a man she had loved, but obviously had never really known.

It wasn't bad enough for him to just up and leave her the way he had three years ago. No, he had to live a secretive second life as a criminal, slinking around, stealing other people's money with his mistress-accomplice.

And the gut-wrenching, slap-in-the-face question was: How could she not have known? The money, the long absences - always explained away - but still, why hadn't she dug deeper, been more observant, less trusting?

A sudden wave of nausea bubbled in her stomach, but she doubled over and swallowed hard against the urge to vomit. She knew throwing up would do nothing to expel the pain. The nausea was a symptom, not the solution.

Sliding her back along the vanity, Sella slumped onto the cold tile floor, pulled the towel from around her wet hair and patted at her dripping face. Then, too tired to walk to her bed, she collapsed into the pile of damp towels around her.

Her life had been a fantasy. Nothing – and no one – was real.

The tears burned again in her eyes and the dark, damp well from which they came seemed cavernous. They rose from the bottom of her soul and erupted into a haunting melody that accompanied the memories of her marriage as the snippets played through her brain.

She wanted to turn the memories off, but of course, she could not; they were imprinted. All she could do was watch as the memories of her fantasy past love with Garrett joined the black residue of the fantasy new love with Drake that she had secretly hoped she had been given by God.

***

It was a Saturday morning in May, 2007 when Garrett walked into her life:

"–I'm new here and everyone says this is the best garage in town." He avoided her brother Phillip who was standing at the battery counter and walked directly over to her as she stood near the till. He was gorgeous, almost pretty in a masculine way, with his defined brow and cheekbones. And those dreamy dark eyes...

"Well, it's the *only* garage in town so-" She had replied awkwardly and then self-consciously smoothed her twill work shirt more neatly into her jeans. They never had strangers show up who looked like this guy.

"Sold. You've convinced me." He smiled that smile. The one that shook the earth under a girl's feet.

"Ha, ha," She smiled back at his charm and sunk deeper into his midnight eyes. Then, embarrassed at herself, she broke the trance and reached for the clipboard with the service checklist, "What do you need done?"

"There you go, being all distracting like that," He continued smiling, proving to her that he wasn't done flirting with her yet, "Now, I've completely forgotten."

"Okay, well-" Never good at banter, Sella blushed and put the clipboard back behind the staplers on the counter in front of her.

"No, I'm just kidding around. I need someone to look at the air conditioning in my truck out there." He gestured towards the Chevrolet pickup parked out front of the shop. Turning his head back around, he said, "I just bought a lake house up here. My name's Garrett. What's yours?"

Less than eight months later:

"-but, Garrett, you want us to elope? What about my parents, my family?"

"I know it may seem sudden to everyone, but we love each other, so why wait? Do you know how long it takes to plan a big wedding? I want you as my wife *now*, Sella, not a year from now."

"–but they will be disappointed. We have so many friends and family that would want to celebrate with us."

"You mean *you* have a lot of family," Garrett said, reminding her again that he had no family to speak of, "But is this wedding about your family or is it about us? I think our wedding should be about us."

"Yes, of course, you're right. It's about us." She said as she put the bridal magazine down, stuffed her disappointment deep inside and melted into his arms.

A few months after their wedding:

"–again? You're going to miss the company Christmas party again? You missed it last year too. Phillip will say something, I know he will. He thinks you intentionally avoid him."

"Your brothers need to lighten up. It's not all about them. Besides, I can't help it, Sella. I have to be in Virginia that weekend."

"This job is turning out to be a lot more travel than you first told me. You're gone almost every week now."

"I know it's turning out that way, but I need this job. Did I tell you that they're talking about a promotion for me in about a month? It will mean I have to be in Virginia a lot more, but the salary increase will be worth it."

"So, you would travel even more?"

"Sella, come on, you know how the game is played. Besides, I need to bring in some serious cash because I've been looking at that house near the river. You said you loved that house, right?"

"But it's so much money, Garrett. We can't possibly afford it."

"Don't worry about money. I can always find the money. I just want to make my wife happy-"

A few months later:

"-a baby? Wow, a baby." He drew back from her suddenly, his eyes darkened with a frown.

"Yes, Garrett. You're excited, aren't you?"

"- uh, yeah. Of course, I am excited. A baby." She thought she heard a hint of excitement in his voice, but she didn't see it reflected in his eyes. It might just take a little time, she told herself, but eventually he would be as excited to be a father as she was to be a mother.

"I think it's a boy," She whispered into his ear as she hugged him close, "and I hope he looks just like his daddy."

When Henri turned four:

"-don't worry, Henri. Daddy will be home in time for your birthday party. Remember, he called you on the telephone to tell you so."

She didn't want to tell her four-year-old that his father had forgotten about the birthday party and only called his son because she had reminded him about it.

"But he said that he would be here for my swimming lessons last night too and he wasn't."

"I know, I'm sorry. He had a meeting come up suddenly and couldn't come home when he expected. That's just daddy's job, Henri. Sometimes he doesn't get to control his schedule."

"I hate his job." Henri pouted as he crashed his toy car into the tires of his toy dump truck.

"Yeah, sometimes I hate it too." She said as she pulled her son towards her and kissed the top of his soft curls.

A few months later:

"–why don't we just move out to Virginia if that's where you have to be all the time!" She slammed the spoon against the counter, sending a mist of spaghetti sauce across the backsplash.

"And make you and Henri leave your family? And you leave your job? No, I couldn't ask that of you. You just have to be patient, Sella. It will get better when I get this next promotion. They are talking about opening an office in the Twin Cities in the next year or so."

"But they expect so much from you, Garrett. And everything is so secretive all the time. I sometimes wonder what kind of company you're working for."

"It's the government side of things that's secretive. You know the way the government has been hacked lately. All these contracts are super classified. You never know who you can trust."

"I guess," She tried to resist the temptation of bitterness, Garrett was just trying to do what he felt was best for their family, "Who would have guessed that selling someone else's stuff could be such a top-secret job?"

"You have no idea."

December 2015: The Christmas before he left them. And now she knew it was the same Christmas that Natalie's car went into the river:

"Garrett, what's wrong? Are you feeling okay?"

"Nothing's wrong." His voice seethed with frustration.

"Well, I just wondered because you were really quiet all day. Henri was so excited for Christmas and you just seemed -absent. Is it work again?"

"Sella, don't nag at me all the time. Yeah, it's work. I've been thinking about work." He looked into her eyes with his statement; something about his look made her feel disposable, like an excess bag and he wanted to lighten his load, "By the way, I have to leave tomorrow."

"But it's the day after Christmas! Can't you just tell them that the chief deal maker is out of commission until after the first of the year?" She remembered that she had tried to joke about it but secretly she was trying to get him to tell her what was really bothering him. But, obviously, Garrett wasn't in the mood for jokes. As quickly as the look of anger shot through his eyes, however, suddenly it was gone, and his "polished" face was back on as he said:

"It doesn't work that way, love. It just doesn't work that way. I'm leaving tomorrow."

A year later, after months of arguments resulting in robotic-motion days and painful nights filled with tears:

"-this isn't working for me any longer, Sella. I've made up my mind and you're not going to change it. You and Henri will be better off without me in the long run." He was adding some clothes to the bag that always sat in his closet with extra sets of clean socks and underwear, never completely unpacked.

"Garrett, you can't really believe that. I love you. Henri needs you."

"I will always take care of Henri. But, Sella, I'm not staying. I need– something else." He said as he tossed in his belt and hairbrush next to his leather toiletries bag.

"You mean *someone* else." She finally said the words, knowing they were true.

"That's not what I said."

"But that's what you meant."

"If it makes you feel better, then, I guess go ahead and believe that." He said harshly as he zipped the bag and stood it on the bedroom floor, pulling up the handle.

"You've changed, Garrett," Her knees buckled and she collapsed onto the side of their bed as her shoulders turned inward and she wiped the tears that showered her cheeks, "This last year, you've really changed. I know there is someone else, I just wish you'd man up and tell me."

"Whatever you want to believe, go ahead. I don't care. I just need to go." He didn't reach out to her, he didn't even look at her as he turned on his heel and strode across the room, pulling his bag behind him.

She watched as he neared their door, realizing with panic that he was leaving her to raise their small son alone. The full extent of that daunting task wasn't clear to her in the moment, however. All she could think of was what would Henri do without his daddy? How would they cope?

But, as soon as the deluge of those worries immersed her, another raw, savage question reared its head, fighting for control of her consciousness.

She didn't want more pain - wasn't this enough? But somehow, something prompted her from deep within. It was now or never, and she had to hear it straight from him.

"Did you ever love me, Garrett?" She asked the question quietly, not even sure at first that he could hear her. But, when he paused at the door, she knew he had. He didn't look her in the eyes, all she had to remember him by was his profile when he said:

"*I don't know.*"

Sella had buried the words in her deepest memory for these past three years.

Her husband didn't know if he ever loved her.

But, if so, why had he persistently pursued her in the beginning of their relationship? Why had he married her? Why tie himself down when he didn't have to?

She'd never gotten answers to any of these questions. She'd been left hanging, in limbo, never believing herself worthy of someone to love and someone to love her back.

Until now. With Drake.

Trouble was, *now* had proven to be no better than *then*.

Drake

Drake shivered in his jacket and flipped the wipers on again to fend off the intermittent, icy rain that drained in rivers down his windshield creating a distorted, misshapen view of the trees alongside the road.

As he drove away from Gisella's house and back towards Twin Shores, he rubbed his throbbing temple with his thumb and begged God, and the empty car, to help him understand the meaning in this whole, futile quest.

"Why did I come here up here in the first place? Of all the guys it could have been, why did it have to be *him*? And why did it have to hurt *her*?"

For a guy so used to handling things, so comfortable taking over and getting things resolved, no matter how many ways Drake tried to examine the situation, there just seemed to be no escape. There was simply no way to settle it and move on from this.

He had lost Gisella before he even had the opportunity to know her.

Although he was surprised by the venom in her wrath, he couldn't blame Gisella for her reaction to the news after hearing what Sheriff Cooper told him earlier.

Cooper knew the man in the photo as Garrett Sommers, a guy who had moved to Twin Shores years before, married Gisella after a whirlwind romance (and against the better judgment of Gisella's close-knit family) and then suddenly up and left Gisella and Henri three years ago without any rational explanation.

As Cooper told him the gut-wrenching story, Drake had been shocked - then angry - then miserable. He sensed somehow that Gisella would mistakenly believe he knew about the affair between Natalie and Garrett and that he had come to Minnesota on some twisted, revenge-filled fishing expedition.

When she opened the door this evening and he looked into her exquisite eyes so filled with joy, he couldn't find words to explain any of this to her. Anything he tried to say to defend himself - that he had no clue, that he'd been as naïve to this relationship as she was – anything that came to mind, sounded self-serving and weak when compared to what she was going through.

For him, the last few weeks had numbed him to the extent of the lies in Natalie's life. But the extent of Garrett's lies – this was a complete shock to Gisella.

Even now after putting together some of the missing pieces of the puzzle, Drake struggled most with one thing: trusting that God was in control. That somehow God knew this was going to happen, and he let it happen anyway.

Drake found himself pleading with God, "Since you are in control, Heavenly Father, would it really hurt to show me a sliver of light on the way forward?"

Unable to see the road now for the tears in his eyes, Drake pulled his car off to the side of the road and leaned his head against the steering wheel. Through his sobs, he continued praying words that spilled into stretches of indecipherable sentences, tethered together by a depth of heartbreak that only God could understand.

A few minutes later, wiping the tears from his face, Drake reached for his cell phone and began typing a text to Gisella, determined not to think too hard about it as his fingers found the words:

Gisella, please believe me when I tell you that I had no idea about the connection between Natalie and your husband. If I had known, I would never have come here and put you in any situation where you would be hurt. I want only the best for you and your family, and I am so sorry to have caused you pain. Please forgive me. – Drake

He didn't expect her to reply. He didn't expect to ever hear from her again, but he felt better for saying it.

Wiping his face once again, hoping that he had cried his last time over this whole ordeal, he shoved the car in drive again and headed forward into his life.

Minnesota was his birthplace and he would surely be back in the state many more times over the course of his life, but he doubted he would ever venture back to the arrowhead region and certainly never back to Twin Shores.

This place and its people were beautiful beyond words, but they haunted him now. And he needed to focus on the future and whatever God put in front of him. Could he do that? Could he really start his life over again and forget about her?

Who knew? But he had to try.

CHAPTER 32

2014

Natalie

I tell this story as I lay dying at the bottom of a river. I don't know if they will find me. At this point, I don't even care if they will find me.

But if they do, they will learn my secrets and I hope when they learn about mine, they will also learn TC's secrets too. I want him to suffer for every single one of them.

But I'm not going to waste any more of my precious time on TC. He doesn't deserve to be in my final thoughts. Because my final thoughts are about me and my life.

It's true what they say, you do evaluate your life at the end. Everyone does.

And my evaluation is this – I am a selfish person and I hurt people. As I think about it, I can't say I've done anything worthwhile with my life. It's been a complete waste of time, which makes me feel like my life was a gift that I threw away without even opening it.

It's a sad thing to say – or more accurately – a sad thought to think, as I lay here dying in this tomb under the ice, but I've reached the end of my life and I don't know what to expect beyond this moment. In fact, everything about this moment completely terrifies me.

Is there a God? I've never thought so. Now, I know - I've been wrong.

There is.

CHAPTER 33

Christmas 2019

Sella & Henri

"Well, at least you got all your sledding out of your system this morning so you could take a bath and warm up before we have to leave for Uncle Phillip's house." His mom said as she scooped up the wet towel and his clothes from the bathroom floor.

"Oh, my gosh, Mom, it was so fun! Did you see that huge drift between the three trees by the garden shed? If you start at the top and kick really hard, you go around a curve like Nascar!" Henri exclaimed as he pulled his favorite fleece sweatshirt over his wet curls. His mom reached around him, lifted a dry towel from the hook and began to dry his hair, pulling his head back and forth in her haste.

"Yes, but you're still shivering. I wish you would have worn your snow pants, Henri. Two pairs of jeans don't keep you dry, you know."

"I know, but I forgot my snow pants at Uncle Phillip's house. I thought the pair of long underwear would help."

"Well, guess not."

As she stood behind him, toweling his hair dry, Henri looked at his reflection in the mirror and made funny faces at himself. Soon finished with his hair, he was just about to escape, when his mom caught at his hand and inspected his fingernails.

"Henri! How long has it been since you clipped your nails?"

"I dunno, a long time, I guess." He mumbled as he noticed the ragged nails. In fact, it had been a long, long time. He couldn't even remember the last time.

"Well, let's go into the living room by the fire so you can get warm. I'll clip them for you. Bring that trash can from under my vanity, please." His mom directed as she left the bathroom with an armload of clothes and towels.

Sitting on the hearth with his back to the crackling fire, Henri waited as his mother pulled the ottoman close to him, positioned the trash can between his legs and took his fingers gently into her hand.

His mom was good at clipping nails, Henri thought as she clipped his thumb nail. She always took her time and never got too close to the skin like what happened almost every time Henri tried to do his own.

As he watched her work, he remembered how Poppy used to sit still while his mom clipped his nails too. Sometimes, he'd tease her and say she got his skin, but she always knew better. His mom would just laugh and tell him not to cry wolf.

"Mom, what did you mean not to cry wolf?" Henri asked, curious about it because he had never been sure what it meant.

"What do you mean?" She paused and raised her eyes, her eyebrows drawn together in confusion.

"When you used to tell Poppy not to cry wolf when you clipped his nails?"

"Oh." His mom's face tightened into the sad look again, and although he had seen it less often lately, he knew that look well, "It's just a story about a boy who always said there was a wolf after him just to get people's attention, but it was never there. Until one time, the wolf really did come after the boy and no one believed him."

"Oh, no. So, you're saying Poppy was teasing you just to get attention?"

"Oh, yeah," She breathed a big sigh as her mouth lifted into a sad smile, "He sure did a lot of that, didn't he?"

"Yeah, he sure did." Henri said, remembering fondly how often his grandfather would tease him too, "I miss him, mom."

"I do too, bud." His mom stopped clipping his nails for a moment as she reached out to straighten some of his curls before she forced a smile that was big enough to see her teeth, making her face really pretty, but still really sad.

"Mom," Henri continued, a question suddenly occurring to him, "do you think Poppy's memory is all better now that he's in heaven?"

"Oh, I should think so." She nodded seriously and went back to work on his fingernails.

That's good, Henri thought. Because Poppy told him all the time how hard it was to lose your memory and Henri was fairly sure that God wouldn't let anyone forget anything in heaven.

As he sat there, patiently waiting for her to finish, another thought popped into his mind that he wanted to ask his mom.

"Mom?"

"Yes?" She raised her eyebrows as she glanced at him.

"Was Poppy teasing me when he said he didn't remember my dad?"

"No, I'm sorry, Henri," She shook her head slowly, "He wasn't teasing. He really couldn't remember your dad. What did he say to you about him?"

"Oh, not much," Henri said as he bounced his knee and then pulled it up under him so he wouldn't be distracted by it, "He sometimes told me that you should get a husband so I could have a dad."

He stopped fidgeting so he could look her straight in the eyes and see her reaction. His grandpa had said that a lot, but he'd never told his mom about it. He didn't want Poppy to get in trouble for not "minding his own business."

"He told you that?" Her brows came together like she was confused, but not really mad.

"Yeah. I told him that I had a dad, but I couldn't remember him very good either."

"Oh, Henri," His mom sighed quietly, as something lit in her eyes, "I'm sorry you can't remember much about your dad. You were so little when he went away."

"It's okay, mom." Henri said, not wanting her to be sad, but still wanting her to know that he had been thinking about something very important and she should know about it because it involved her too, "I've been thinking though. It sure would be nice someday to have a dad. I would like to talk to a dad about stuff."

"What kind of stuff?" She turned her head to the side as she listened intently.

Okay, she seemed really interested, he thought, so he kept going.

"Oh, you know. Stuff. Like fishing and shaving and other guy stuff."

"Well," She replied slowly as she considered his words, "I can talk to you about fishing. And shaving?" She turned his cheek and peered closely at his face before backing away and smiling, "Well, I think you have a few years before you need to talk to someone about that."

"Yeah, but someday, you will get married and I will get a dad, right?" Henri knew that the reasons he'd given her were just excuses to have a dad. She had seen right through him. Truth was, he really just *wanted* a dad around; he didn't really know *why* he wanted it.

"Yeah, maybe someday that could happen." Trying to end the discussion, she reached for his other hand and started with his thumb nail.

He knew it was a stretch and she might get upset, thinking he wasn't "minding his own business," but Henri spoke quietly to his mother's hair as she bent her head close to his hand.

"I used to talk to Drake like a dad."

She looked up suddenly, her eyes wide.

"Have you talked to Drake lately?" She asked slowly, with a voice that always made Henri a little nervous.

"Not since you got mad at him." Henri replied honestly, glad he hadn't emailed Drake any more fishing videos since he left Twin Shores at the time of Poppy's funeral. His mom had told him that she and Drake had a disagreement and that they shouldn't talk to him anymore. Henri didn't know what had happened, but from the look on his mom's face, he knew better than to ask too many questions.

"Well," His mom breathed in deeply and let her breath out slowly as she looked him in the eyes, an expression on her face that he hadn't seen before, "I'm not mad at him anymore."

His heart lifted immediately, and he couldn't help smiling and bouncing up from the hearth in excitement, "Really? Does that mean you will be his friend again? And I can talk to him again about fishing?"

"We'll see, Henri."

That was all his mom said. She didn't nod her head Yes or shake her head No. She didn't agree or disagree.

Henri knew his mom - that look meant she could go either way. She had what Poppy called a "good poker face."

But something about the look in her eyes and the smile that showed her teeth gave him hope and Henri said a quick thank you prayer in his head.

Now would be the moment when a grown-up would stop talking and let her think about it, not push too hard, Henri admonished himself in his mind.

Besides, he was fairly sure that since she hadn't said "No," then his mom was still thinking and praying about it.

Now would be the time when a grown-up would say, *let God take care of it.*

So, Henri didn't ask his mom anything else about a dad, or about Drake.

***

Sella sat on the rock and pushed her boots deeper into the glistening snow drift at her feet. Shoving her mittened hands into the pockets of her down jacket, she pushed her shoulders back and breathed in the sharp sting of the winter breeze.

What a beautiful Christmas day. The river was enchanting this time of year, with the muted shades of tree trunks punching through the iridescent drifts along the bank and brown and merlot-colored shrubbery mounded with caked snow as if someone had dolloped too much icing on them.

Between the rugged riverbanks, a wide trail of rolling snowdrifts rested on large patches of ice and glistened like stars in the sunlight, hiding the slow-churning river beneath them. A peaceful covering, the white blanket of drifts stood pristine, interrupted only by the tracks of animals crisscrossing across the ice patches from one side of the river to the other.

Removing a twig that had gotten lodged in between her snow pants and her boot, Sella turned her head to study the tracks she had left in the snow as she approached the riverbank. Deep in the snow, large by comparison to the animal tracks, her imprint was distinct and unmistakable.

A person might be tempted to think you could hide out here in the woods, she mused, but that wasn't true. You will always leave a mark. You can never really hide. Eventually, you are forced to ask yourself, what are you hiding from?

She had thought long and hard about everything that had happened between her and Garrett. Over the past few weeks, with the help of Coop and her brothers, she had pieced together where he had come from and what he truly was.

And, after all that she learned, she was still left with the question, what could she do to redeem him? And why should she feel obligated to do so?

Yes, he was Henri's father, but Garrett had willingly sacrificed that treasured responsibility years ago. Yes, he had been her husband, but he had cared even less for that role.

Would she allow Garrett to define her life forever? Could she allow him to define Henri's life that way?

Or, instead, was she ready, with the steady presence of God by her side, to finally – finally – let him, let *it*, all go?

Hearing a low gurgling sound, Sella sat forward on the boulder and glanced over the riverbank at the drift-covered river. Below her feet, she was surprised to find a swirl of the darkest, coal-black water she'd ever seen. It was moving along, protected by a wind-blown crescent of snowbank that from the top looked solid but was instead a false floor of snow, tenting over the stream below.

There. See? You may think you're hiding under the thick cover you show everyone, but you're not fooling anyone. You can't stop life by hiding from it.

Life is always moving. It's time to get in it and swim.

With a tentative smile, Sella tossed the twig into the hole where the water tumbled it under and popped it back up again, carrying it away to a hidden place further down river.

Pulling her mitten off, Sella reached into her pocket for her cell phone and dialed.

***

"–So, when do you think you're going to move?" Drake's sister Miranda asked as she passed the steaming bowl of mashed potatoes over her six-year-old daughter Nina's blonde head and set it on the table between Drake and his brother-in-law Caleb.

"Nothing is set in stone yet, we're still talking through how it all would look." Drake hedged, wanting to manage his family's expectations. The plan to split the functions of Connor-Denning Security into two offices, one in Chicago and one in Minneapolis, was tentatively on schedule to complete by early spring, but there was always the chance something could delay it.

"But you are definitely planning on moving back to Minnesota, right?" His mother paused with the plate of dinner rolls held in mid-air, as her sharp gaze pinned him to his chair.

"Yes, yes. That's the plan, we're just not–" Drake stopped mid-sentence as his phone buzzed in the back pocket of his jeans.

The people around the table quieted, knowing that in his line of work, if Drake was receiving a call on Christmas day, it must be serious, and it usually wasn't good news.

Gisella. The phone display read in distinct, light blue lettering.

Sitting back in his chair, never expecting to hear from her again, he stared at his phone dumbfounded for a moment as it rang a second time and then a third time.

"Well?" His dad prompted, waving his hand towards Drake's phone, "You going to take that?"

Yeah, I'm going to take it.

Drake pushed the chair back from the table and strode into the living room of the century-old farmhouse, pausing once he reached the window that looked out over his parents' back yard and the corn fields beyond, now shrouded beneath waves of snow drifts.

What was he going to say to her? These would be the first words he'd spoken to her since he threw a hand grenade into her life a month ago.

He swiped open the call and waited for a moment, his heart pounding and his hand shaking as he brought the phone to his ear. Closing his eyes, he pictured her face that awful night the last time he saw her, and his gut wrenched at the painful memory.

"Hello, Drake?" Her voice spoke into the silence, "It's me, Sella."

As soon as he heard her voice a sense of peace rushed over him, like a floodgate had been opened and he was drowning in it. Like he couldn't swim to the top and he didn't care. Like he could float along in this feeling forever.

"Hello, Gisella," As he said her name, his voice, buoyant with unadulterated joy also sounded confident, even to him. Where was this coming from? How could he be so confident in a future with her after what had happened between them? And what had happened between their exes?

But, even given all of that, here he was on the phone with her. He didn't know how and he didn't know why, but for some reason, she was calling him on her own terms and he was sure she wouldn't do that unless she was thinking the same way he was.

She was his future. And he was hers.

"Gisella," He repeated her name slowly as he closed his eyes and took a deep breath, allowing the moment to stretch wide enough to feel all that had happened before and dream about all that was yet to come, "I've been waiting for your call."

The End

If you enjoyed this J. Marie novel, you are bound to enjoy reading others! Take a peek at the following book summaries for the other three J. Marie novels – They are all available on Amazon.com in e-book and paperback versions.

For more information on the author and what she's writing, go to <u>www.jmariebooks.com</u> or find J. Marie Books on Facebook and Instagram

Find Your Way Home
by J. Marie

.... those people and places. None of them seemed real anymore. It's like that day his grandparents came in June, he packed up all he had. And it all fit in a duffel bag....

Where are you supposed to go when you're a thirteen-year-old city kid, your mom has just been thrown in jail for a repeat DUI drug charge, and you've never even met the man who is your father? You certainly can't count on your mom's latest drug dealer boyfriend to offer any support – he's basically kicking you to the curb, making it abundantly clear he couldn't care less what happens to you.

A story of faith for today, Find Your Way Home is a tale of friendship and family, portraying the life of Elliott, a troubled young teen learning to deal with his lot in life. Through his personal, soul searching inner voice, the reader is brought into his world which is darkened by the effects of his mother's drug and alcohol addiction and the physical abuse at the hands of her boyfriend. Even though, at first, he doesn't see it as such, his saving grace is found in his grandparents' insistence that he live with them on their rural Minnesota farm while his mother serves her time in prison and state-mandated treatment program.

It's in the quaint, lakeside town of Lake Belle, Minnesota near his grandparents' farm, that Elliott crosses paths with the Eastman kids, Daniel and his sister Lauryn. To Elliott, the Eastman kids embody everything he is not – where his life is filled with chaos and dysfunction, their lives seem to be easy and carefree, almost "perfect."

Over the months, and then years, we witness as the Eastman's accept him as their "other brother" and a deep friendship develops between the three children, with an especially poignant bond between Elliott and Lauryn. Elliott begins to see that their "perfect" life isn't so perfect after all, seeing firsthand the marital problems of Todd and Gabrielle and the effect it has on his friends, especially Lauryn.

As the years pass, the kids begin pursuing their unique interests, taking them in different directions. Elliott, having always embraced computer gaming as a means of escape, turns his boyhood passion into a small business and then into a career, which takes him far from Lake Belle, but leaves him unsatisfied and in an endless search for happiness, home and family. Lauryn, always certain that Lake Belle is home, is simply searching for, and thinks she may have finally found in Gabe, a local craftsman, the "right" someone to share it with.

When a series of life events suddenly forces Elliott to acknowledge his deep-seated feelings of shame and resentment over his mother's decade-long battle with addiction, and a soul-searching recognition of his true feelings considering marriage and his future, he finally discovers what family, home, and love really means.

A Promised Place -- A Love Story, Continued
by J. Marie

Fifty years separate their lives, fifty years separate their stories, but one house and a similar, soul-searching journey unite them.

You might have already met Lauryn and Elliott in J. Marie's first novel *Find Your Way Home*, but if not, you are sure to become friends with them in this new novel *A Promised Place*.

Although the story continues where the first novel left off, *A Promised Place* stands uniquely on its own with its tender story of holding fast to love through the tough times and the search for a deeper faith through the midst of it.

When Lauryn Grant purchases the house at 316 Promise Place in Rivers Bend, Minnesota, she finds an enticing project to add to the list of home renovations featured on her website and in her social media. While she's aware that the house has an interesting history, she finds the most intriguing story is written in a journal that has been hidden in a secret place inside the house for fifty years, just waiting to be discovered.

The journal that she finds tells the story of a simple, small-town man with a past life that doesn't quite fit the rigid constructs of his present one. Unexpectedly, Lauryn finds his captivating story not only influences how she deals with struggles in her life and with her faith, but it also has the power to change her forever.

The Forgotten House
by J. Marie

Death may silence your voice, but your spirit lives on in the ones still here, the ones you left behind.

Trouble is, now these people must piece together all the tasks you've left unfinished and all the words you've left unsaid. With your abrupt departure, they find that you didn't quite take care of everything. Thankfully, you left a note. It's just too bad you weren't more specific...

When literary and film legend JL McMichael dies suddenly of a heart attack, his family, colleagues and fans are devastated and mourn his passing, appreciating the incredible impact his work has had on a generation. But, living life as a legend isn't always easy, and sometimes even legends fall short, especially with those closest to them, their family.

With his passing, the writer's son Canton and daughter Jasmine, both active in their father's business empire, become the primary beneficiaries of his sizeable estate, including his multiple residences across the country. But, of course, there is also his granddaughter Mallory, his youngest son Parker's daughter, to consider.

His responsibility ever since a tragic car accident took her parents' lives over ten years earlier, JL McMichael's estranged granddaughter Mallory is beneficiary of his writing get-away, a little stone house in Minnesota. To Mallory, this inheritance – a house so insignificant that the family forgot he even owned it - feels like the final, spite-filled blow in the tumultuous battle of wills between the enigmatic literary legend and his headstrong granddaughter.

Upon her arrival in Minnesota, Mallory finds that The Forgotten House holds some traumatic memories of her life with her grandfather, but it also holds some tantalizing secrets outlined in a letter he wrote to her, but never delivered. This letter, inspired by the intriguing next-door neighbor, propels her on a journey that could change everything.

AUTHOR BIO

J. Marie is the author of four inspirational novels including FIND YOUR WAY HOME (March 2018 Amazon), THE FORGOTTEN HOUSE (October 2018 Amazon), A PROMISED PLACE (November 2019 Amazon) and THOSE WE LOVE and What They Hide (November 2020 Amazon).

Many of the characters and the experiences of her characters can be traced to people in her life growing up in southwestern Minnesota. Her faith in God, her husband, their family, and friends are all sources of inspiration for the stories she hears in her head and happily shares with readers who are searching for wholesome, heart-warming novels that depict sometimes flawed, imperfect people living out their faith.

BOOK CLUB DISCUSSION QUESTIONS

1. Like many people, the characters in this book struggled with their faith during trying times in their lives. List some examples you found in the novel. Did they resolve those struggles?

2. Can you describe Drake's personality in the beginning of the novel and how he changed as the novel went along? How did his faith impact the arc of this character?

3. Can you describe Sella's character in the beginning of the novel and how she changed as the novel went along?

4. How did meeting Sella affect Drake's character in the novel?

5. What would be your one-word descriptor for Drake and Sella's relationship?

6. Did Natalie have any redeeming qualities? What were they? What realizations did she come to understand at the end of her story?

7. Did you see the connections between the characters coming or were you surprised? What clues did you find that made you suspect the connection?

8. What overarching themes did you identify in the novel? Can you give examples of how the characters exemplified, lived out, these themes in their lives?

9. How did the setting of the novel enhance the story line?

10. Have you had someone close to you struggle with a memory condition like Luca? How did you relate to the struggles Sella and her family had to deal with as they cared for her elderly father?

11. What surprised you about the novel?

12. Take a moment to reflect on the title Those We Love and What They Hide. Why do you think the author chose that as the title?

Made in the USA
Middletown, DE
02 September 2021